NORTH BEAT CHRISTMAS

BOOK 3

THE BEAT STREET SERIES

Jenna Zark

PRINT ISBN 978-1-77400-073-1
EPUB ISBN 978-1-77400-074-8

This is a work of fiction. Names, characters, places, brands, media, and incidents are either the product of the author's imagination or are used fictitiously. Any resemblance to similarly named places or to persons, living or deceased, is unintentional. In addition, narrative language and dialogue was designed to evoke the 1950s. The author does not condone 1950s language in present times.

www.dragonmoonpress.com

To my family, and all those who believe
art has the power to heal.

CONTENTS

Jenna Zark

ACKNOWLEDGMENTS

NORTH BEAT CHRISTMAS and the Beat Street series are dedicated to the memory of Susan Jeffers Casel, for pushing me to write this story and making sure I followed through on it—and for being an unforgettable presence in my life.

I am also grateful to Ellen Byron, Kim Hines, Rita Itzkowitz and Janet Stilson for their careful reading and insightful comments, and to Pam Labbe, who works tirelessly to connect my books with readers.

A special thank you is due to therapist Laurie Endris, MSW, LICSW, for her expertise in helping me to better understand Marty's condition. Another thank you goes out to my excellent editor Sandra Nguyen.

Lastly, I want to thank cover artist/publisher Gwen Gades at Dragon Moon Press for her outstanding artistry and dedication to authors.

1

CALIFORNIA EMERGENCY

I'VE BEEN TRYING to call my father for the last hour, but he won't pick up the phone—even when I call and let it ring fifty times. Most people pick up the phone if you ring ten times, but not Gary Daddy-o. I think—I mean I *know* he's got a bad case of the Blues. We call them Sads. I keep calling because we're in New York and he's in California, and from everything my brother says, Gary Daddy-o's world has fallen apart.

"Ruby?" my mother calls. "Wanna have dinner?"

"In a minute," I tell her.

"What ya doin' in there?"

"Noth—I'm fine! Be right there, Nell-mom," I say, hanging up the phone. Except the last thing I want is dinner. It's a week before school lets out for the holidays, and all I can think about is getting out to California. Gary Daddy-o didn't invite us, but I can't just bop around New York while he sits in his room in San Francisco. I want to tell Nell-mom we have to go out there, and she needs to understand it's not just any Christmas. It's a big deal.

Because my dad was living in Washington, D. C. with his fiancée, Maddie, and their wedding date was supposed to be October 11, 1958. I'm pretty sure they would have invited my brother Ray and me for either Christmas or New Year's, and it would have been easy enough to go. But they split up before Halloween, and then just a couple weeks ago, Gary Daddy-o took off for California. When my Daddy-o has the blues, he can overdo it with alcohol, which I'm not supposed to say, but I'm saying it anyway.

That's the main reason Ray and I need to convince Nell-mom to let us go out west and get our stepfather Chaz to pay for it.

Nell-mom came here when she was sixteen, but I don't know why, and she never told me her real age—I had to find that out from my dad. My mom came on a Greyhound bus and wound up living with two artist ladies who were on that same bus with her. She doesn't talk about it much, though—so it's hard to find out why she dropped out of high school in Sheboygan, Wisconsin to come to the city all alone.

Nell-mom just finished drying the dishes I washed, and Ray's making coffee for the three of us. I'm allowed a half cup, which seems ridiculous for a twelve-year-old, but I can usually sneak up to a cup and gulp it down if no one's looking—and they usually don't. Ray's sixteen and that means he can have two cups—again, unfair. On the other hand, I've got a lot of fish to fry and it's time to get started. The main thing I need to do is prove it's okay for me to go cross-country on a train with my brother. I can't take no for an answer.

I call my mother and father Nell-mom and Gary Daddy-o because that's what I've always called them. One day I may graduate to their first names, because we're Beats and the Beat Generation isn't supposed to be hung up on stuff like what you call your parents. Nell-mom didn't used to act that much like a parent, but ever since I got taken away from her by a social worker and she had to switch her life around to get me back, she's been a lot more *mom* than anyone needs. Gary Daddy-o is the opposite.

"Why did you move here?" I ask. Nell-mom looks away, and I can tell she's trying to make up something. She twirls a strand of curly, coppery-brown hair in her fingers until I smell the shampoo she uses. Her hair smells like lilacs, which Gary Daddy-o said was part of what makes her "beautiful and mysterious." Nell-mom's blue eyes and freckles make her look sunny and friendly. She *can* be sunny when she wants, but if she's mad at you, she can whip up a storm pretty quickly. And like most mothers, she only tells you what she wants you to know. If she's got a secret, you'll never know it, no matter how hard you try to find out.

Before I can ask again about New York, Nell-mom

starts talking. "I knew I was an artist, and Greenwich Village is the place for artists to be."

Okay, I think, *now we're getting somewhere.*

"But you were still in school. Weren't you?"

"Ruby," she says. "Why are you asking me about this?"

I decide to bite the bullet and explain.

"You know Gary Daddy-o's going to be alone in San Francisco this Christmas," I say. "We want to visit him for a little while." Nell-mom sighs and crosses her arms. Ray starts pouring water into the coffee pot, but he's staring so hard at us I'm surprised he isn't spilling it all over the kitchen counter.

"Yeah," says Nell-mom. "I know. But I thought he was in Washington—"

Now it's my turn to keep secrets. I can't prove it and don't say this out loud, but I'm almost positive Maddie broke up with Gary Daddy-o. It could have been a money thing, because it seemed to me she had most of it and he might not have been bringing in very much.

Nell-mom, on the other hand, got married to my stepfather Chaz and nobody minds that he's the breadwinner. I guess that's what men are supposed to do? It seems pretty stupid, especially when everybody knows they can't handle money anyway. Gary Daddy-o can't—and lost two women who were really important to him because of it. I just feel like he must be a mess right now—which must be why he's not picking up the phone.

Gary Daddy-o went to San Francisco to play bass in a friend's band, but now the friend is on tour and my dad can only stay at his place in a neighborhood called North Beach until March. It's supposed to be like Greenwich Village on the West Coast, with mostly hipsters. Gary Daddy-o calls it "North Beat."

There may or may not be work for Gary Daddy-o when his pal gets back, but he's probably going to have to move out, no matter what. I don't know what he'll do then, but I'm hoping he'll move back to Greenwich Village and start playing music again with his friends Les and Bo.

Right now, though, school is ending for the holidays on December 12 and won't start again until the Monday after New Year's Day, which gives me and Ray plenty of time to get out to the west coast by train, stay through Christmas, and go back home a few days later. When I tell Nell-mom about our plans, she says, "I don't love the idea of you two traveling alone."

"We're not alone!" I say. "Les and Bo can go with us as far as Chicago. They're going to see Bo's grandmother for Christmas and New Year's, and then all we'll have to do is change trains and go the rest of the way by ourselves. There's just one train to San Francisco from Chicago, so we wouldn't have to do anything after we get on it except eat, sleep, talk or read and then get off at the end of the ride."

Nell-mom sighs again. "Who's paying your way?"

"Well, Chaz says he will if you say yes."

"I see," she answers.

"The main thing I want to explain is that Ray and I are being responsible, just by asking if we can see our dad," I say.

Nell-mom squints as she looks at me. "Responsible?"

"Because we're not sneaking away—"

"Like you did when your friend Sophie went out to Chicago?" she asks.

"I was super worried about my friend," I say. "And that's not what we're doing now—"

"It better not be," she replies.

"It's totally different!" I try to match her voice and sound like a parent. "You have Chaz and your friends here, while Gary Daddy-o has no one, and he was just thrown out of someone's life for the second time in less than a year." Saying that makes Nell-mom look down at the floor, and I hope it makes her feel guilty, since she was the person who started all this.

I realize most kids want their parents to stay together, and I don't think they have any idea what it's like when they don't and you have to chase them all over the country. Parents are crazy and always have been. Nell-mom probably gets what I'm saying, but doesn't want to admit it. She still has to understand that Gary Daddy-o shouldn't be left alone.

Not that Gary Daddy-o *has* to be alone. You can see how ladies smile at him when he's playing bass in a club like the Village Gate. I think Nell-mom would have stayed with him forever, but they couldn't get married because he never divorced his first wife who married him because she was pregnant. They lost touch when there was a miscarriage, and the first wife disappeared.

I'm betting Gary Daddy-o would have gotten a divorce sooner, but couldn't find that wife for years.

The thing is that in our family, everybody was cool with it. Nell-mom only got married in order to spring me from the children's home, where the social worker Mrs. Levitt sent me because she thought we didn't have a proper family atmosphere.

It ended up with Nell-mom leaving Gary Daddy-o to marry Chaz, which I hated, but what can you do? By the time Gary Daddy-o found the first lady he married and divorced her, it was too late for him and Nell-mom to be together again.

All this is way too complicated, I know. It was the social worker's fault, mainly, and part of me still hasn't forgiven her, even though I kind of did last summer, but that's a whole other story that really doesn't matter anymore.

Whatever else I mess up tonight, I've got to keep talking until Nell-mom gives up and lets Ray and me go to San Francisco.

"You're going to be so busy anyway, getting ready for your show at Chaz's gallery. Right?" I say. "If Ray and I are out of your hair, you'll be able to get a lot more done before the show. You won't have to cook or clean or go grocery shopping. The only thing you'll have to do is paint."

Nell-mom looks at me, and I can tell by her eyes she wants to agree.

"Les and Bo will be with us every second until we're in Chicago," I say. "Right, Ray?"

"True," Ray says. "They can even walk us to our other train and be sure we get on it—"

"And Ray and I know how to get around—we're

not going to let anybody put something over on us," I add.

"I get all that," Nell-mom starts to say, and I can tell she's looking for an excuse to keep us home and I better interrupt her.

"One thing I learned on that trip to Chicago was how to be careful. I mean Ray's girlfriend and I were fine, going out and coming back—"

"The only problem Ruby had was forgetting to ask permission," Ray points out. I guess he's trying to be helpful.

Nell-mom's eyes get sharp all of a sudden and I kick my brother under the table. *Why does he always bring things up that get me in trouble?*

Ray looks over at me and says, "Oh!" and then turns back to Nell-mom. "Not that Ruby's going to do anything like that ever again, are you, Rubes?" he asks.

"Never," I say, "And as soon as you said you wanted me home, I came right back—"

"You came right back because I was furious," Nell-mom says.

"I'm twenty thousand times more mature now than I was then! I'll be thirteen in four months which means I'll be a teenager. I could have gotten *married* in the Middle Ages," I reply.

"Ruby," Nell-mom says, but she's starting to laugh and both of us know it.

"What I mean is I'm going to be an adult in about two minutes and Ray practically is, already—"

"I wish Les and Bo were going all the way across—"

"It's a hop, skip and jump from Chicago to San

Francisco. And they'll even meet us at the station on the way back so we can all go together to New York right after New Year's." I'm kinda-sorta deciding this before I talk to Les and Bo, but I figure they'd go along with it and it doesn't hurt to throw out the idea and see if it lands.

Nell-mom doesn't say anything, and I can tell she's thinking.

"This is the only way to see Gary Daddy-o," I say. And it's the only chance we'll ever have to see California."

"We could all go out there together some time," Nell says.

I frown. "This is a family thing. We need to go now."

"I know, but—" Nell-mom frowns, too.

At this point, I know I have to keep talking. Sometimes, you just need to keep chit-chatting until someone gives up and lets you do what you want.

"You said you knew you were an artist, right?" I ask.

"Yeah, so?"

I start telling her about the famous bookstore Inner Pages, which is supposed to be in North Beach where Gary Daddy-o lives. They publish a whole lot of Beat poets— and everybody who knows *me* knows how much I want to write poetry, too.

I should tell you Beats (*not* Beatniks, by the way) really, really care about art. Because artists want to dig a little deeper into what makes us tick. I mean humans, not just Beats.

"I bet you knew when you were my age you wanted to grow up and be a painter," I say. "And I hope that means—" I stop, trying to think about what to say next.

"What?" Nell-mom says.

"You should see how important it is for me to go to places like Inner Pages, since poems are really important to me. There's no time like now and if I wait to see Inner Pages, I might never see it. But that's not the main reason," I add. "It's about Gary Daddy-o."

Ray nods, and says, "Exactly," which is all he's good for, I guess. Nell-mom stares out the window at the flashing lights of a fire truck blaring its siren. They're exactly right to blare, since what we're in the middle of is a California emergency that's as bad as any fire in the city of New York.

"Okay," says Nell-mom. I sit up straight like she always wants me to.

"Does that mean yes? You'll let us go out there?"

"Thanks, Mom!" Ray says, and I get up and reach out to hug her.

"You are the bestest," I say, but then Nell-mom shakes her head and stands up.

"What's wrong now?" I say.

"I am saying you can go."

"Great!" I shout, but she puts up her hand.

"But everything you say about this trip better be true, Ruby! And it all has to go the way you say it will." Nell-mom looks at me hard and straight, without blinking. She wants me to know she means business. "You hear me?"

I look up at her, promising with my eyes to be the kid I never was. The one who listens and does exactly what she says. "Every word."

2

HOPE TRAIN

THERE'S HOPE RUNNING up and down this train, so fresh you can almost taste it. I know it's because of Christmas—what else would it be? Gary Daddy-o used to say it's the most hopeful time of year, and that made us hopeful, too. People are walking down the aisles lugging presents for grandchildren, or holding little kids on their laps. Sometimes the kids are cranky until their moms give them a piece of candy, which makes the crank disappear.

A group of couples at the front end of the train is singing Christmas carols, which would normally make me want to jump out the window, but it doesn't today. The whole train is noisy and dirty, but when we pull out of Penn Station and leave the tunnel part, the sun starts pouring in the windows and people start clapping, which makes Ray and me start laughing like someone's tickling us. I like seeing Ray that way, since I think he misses his girlfriend Jo-Jo. They see each other every other minute, but Ray says when you're in love with someone, it's never enough.

Jo-Jo's mom said she couldn't go with Ray and me, but I just feel lucky we got Nell-mom to say yes. Les and Bo are sitting right across from us, since they were the reason we got to make this trip at all. Everyone's in a good mood right now, including me.

Les is telling Bo he can't wait to eat his grandmother's Christmas dinner, and Bo allows that she's the best cook in Chi-town. Les describes not only the pork roast, but all the side dishes Bo's grandmother makes, like candied yams, black-eyed peas, and corn bread, until I have to stop my mouth from watering. I ask Les what they had at his house at Christmas when he was growing up, and he says, "Nothing you'd want," and we all laugh this time. I know Les was rich, but whatever he's said about his family isn't very good. He talks about Christmases where his dad was out very late and no one knew where he was, and his mother was in her room crying and then threw things at his dad when he finally did get home. I try not to ask him a lot of questions, because I hate when people ask about stuff I don't want to talk about. Besides, if Les is anything, he's someone who wants to be happy, always. "Life is short," he always says.

We play Go Fish, Rummy and Pinochle. We play

so many different games I can't remember them all, but you can't win at cards with Bo unless he's on your team. When we're tired of cards, we play guessing games about movie stars, and I win most of them because I read so many movie magazines.

Then Les asks if everybody's hungry and we go to the dining car, which is an adventure in itself. I don't know how the waiters pour coffee and hit your cup instead of your head, but they do. We talk and eat and drink the Cokes Les buys for us, and then back in our seats we play cards again. But when it starts getting darker, we each try to sleep in our seats. I remember Sophie saying it's hard, but I had no idea *how* hard. Still, I try to do it because I don't want to wake anyone else up on the train.

Most everyone has gotten pretty quiet, and I close my eyes tight and try to remember the fairy-tales Nell-mom told me at bedtime, but that doesn't work. Neither does counting sheep or listening to the sounds of the train as it moves further and further across the country. I try counting backwards, and after a little while I think I do sleep, because when I wake up it's starting to get light again.

We go to the dining car for breakfast, but when we come back, I'm not in the mood for games. For one thing, my neck feels a little stiff from sitting up all night, trying to sleep. I think I need what Ray calls a distraction to feel better. I ask Bo to tell us about growing up in Alabama, because he's the best storyteller I've ever heard, even though he's a musician. He could be a storyteller too, but there's no money in it.

"We grew up being tight with each other," Bo says, locking the fingers on each hand together to show how close the people were in his town. "There was a woman everybody used to go to when they got sick. She cured my daddy of a disease that swelled up his arm to the size and color of a pumpkin, using plant juice and castor oil. She wouldn't take money, but liked me to sing to her, like I did in church. She even talked the pastor into giving me a solo."

Now and again Les chimes in with how *his* mother wanted him to take piano lessons. "Mother got mad when I decided to play saxophone instead," Les says, and then Bo talks about the first time he picked up a guitar. "I knew right then I wasn't going to do anything else, no matter what."

"Didn't that man come from Alabama, that guitar fella?" Les asked.

"You mean the man who sold his soul to the devil so he could play like nobody's business?"

"That's an old legend," Ray points out, but Bo stops him.

"Old or not, I met him. And if the devil asked me to sell him my soul if he could make me play better? I'd say yes, too."

"Did he tell you—" I stop before I can finish.

"What?" Bo asks.

"Did he say what the devil looked like?" I know it's a dumb question, and Ray snorts to tell me that. But I still want to know.

"He looks different every time," Bo answers quickly, and I love him for taking me seriously.

"And the real devil don't usually help you with guitar," Bo says. "He's a whole lot better at putting ugly stuff into people's heads. Telling them people like me aren't as good as white people. Putting up signs that say "For Whites Only" outside restaurants and bars and even barber shops. Growing up and trying to vote in the South was an adventure I don't even want to think about—but that's why I went to Alabama to march last summer. So I could help more people vote like they wanted to."

"What was it like there?" I asked.

"People gathered on the streets where we were marching," Bo says, "Only it wasn't to help us." Crowds of people were spitting at the marchers and calling them "dirty coloreds" and other names Nell-mom warned us never to use, or we'd be grounded. We never would anyway, because Ray and I know there's nothing cool about an ugly word—and we know those words when we see them.

Les looks down at his hands and then pushes a big strand of blonde hair back off his forehead. I can't help but wonder what he's thinking. It looks like Bo's wondering too, because all of a sudden his story takes a turn and we all jump to a new chapter. "But you know," he says, "There were white people marching with us, too, and one of them's right here in front of you."

Les doesn't look at us, but Ray says he knows that, even though I didn't.

"Proudest day of my life," Bo says, "when I saw my friend standing up with me. With me and for me. There's nothing he could do would come even close to that—just to show me how much he cared about me."

"Me and Ray care, too," I said.

"That goes without saying, honey," says Bo.

I sit up a little straighter, because when Bo talks about stuff like this it always makes me feel like something *important* is happening, and that *I'm* important enough to know about it. I want us all to keep talking, but we're starting to get close to Chicago, which means we'll have to leave this train. Everybody starts pulling on their suitcases and putting on hats and makeup, and I hunt around for my notebook, which fell through the cracks between seats and onto the floor. Luckily, I find it. That notebook is my life.

When we pull into the station, Les and Bo get their instruments from the shelves near our seats and we all get off the train. Les buys us tuna and cheese sandwiches from a pushcart in the station hall. They walk us down to where our train's supposed to be and wait for it with us, just like they promised Nell-mom. Then, Bo leans over and says something that takes me by surprise.

"I hope you have a good Christmas with your daddy," Bo says. "When you work together on songs and play together, you get to know someone pretty good. Your dad's an old friend, and there's nothing Les and I won't do for him. And he's done for us, too. But if anything happens and you want to talk to somebody, or you need help, I want you to take my grandmother's number." Bo asks for my notebook and borrows Les's pen, which he usually keeps in the pocket of his camel-hair coat. Bo carefully writes down a phone number on a piece of paper, his long, lean fingers making each number easy to read, like a piece of music. Next, he tears out another piece of paper and writes the number down again and this time he hands it to Ray. "I want both of you to have it."

"S'gonna be all right, Bo," says Les, and Bo says he *knows* it's going to be all right, but he *still* wants us to have his number.

"Thanks, man," says Ray, and they sort of hug like guys do, which isn't a hug, really; it's more of a tap-tap on the shoulder, but it's their way of telling each other everything's okay, I guess. Then Les gives me a real hug, and so does Bo. I shove Bo's number in my pocket and put my notebook away before getting on the train.

Ray says Chaz paid for a sleeper car on this portion of the trip, which suits me fine because I'm exhausted. Before we try to find it, I turn to the window and wave at Les and Bo, who stand there smiling at us. I look around to see if there's anyone waving around us, but most people are concentrating on finding their seats and Ray tells me to hurry. He's already hustling down the aisle and I have to run to keep up, while my suitcase bangs into my ankles and people glare at me when they're going the opposite way.

By the time we finally get to the sleeper car, I squinch inside and sit down on the bottom bed next to Ray. It's the tiniest room I've ever seen, but at least there's beds in it, which is all I'm really interested in anyway. I'm not exactly sure where we're going to eat our sandwiches, but Ray thinks I should climb up to the top bunk and eat my lunch up there. Of course that gives him the window, but that's brothers for you. At the same time, I'm not going to eat my sandwich on the top of some itty bitty little bunk. I tell him I'm going to the dining car, and he can come, too, if he wants.

"What if they make you order, like you're in a restaurant?" he asks.

"We'll just get some drinks and dessert," I say. "I'm getting thirsty anyway."

We make our way to the dining car, but have to pass through a smoking car first, which makes me cough the whole time we're in it. I have no idea why, but the air all over this train feels staler than the first one. We eat our sandwiches in the dining car while a group of guys who seem like they're in college sing, "For He's a Jolly Good Fellow" and one of them sits there, trying not to look embarrassed. Ray and I get some ginger ale and split a piece of chocolate cake, which is so good I immediately wish we could have another one.

The day goes by more or less like the last two, except there's no Les and Bo. We look out the window a lot, and it's amazing how big and flat the country is for a while and then how mountains start showing up in Colorado. They're so beautiful, all you can do is stare. I do that until it gets dark, but then I start wishing Les and Bo were still here or that we'd gotten off the train with them and stayed in Chicago.

Which is crazy, right? I mean, I'm going somewhere that's supposed to be one of the most magical cities in the world. I'm going to see my dad, and visit a famous bookstore with famous poets running in and out of it. Plus, it's Christmas, the season of hope. Except what Bo said about calling him if we needed help sounded kind of scary, even though I know he didn't mean it to be. I don't want to call him and don't want a reason to.

I close my eyes tight again, trying to count backwards. *Christmas is coming, Christmas is coming,* I repeat over and over and over again. The train wheels answer, rumbling, with the very same words.

3

SHOESHINE

WE'RE AT THE Sixteenth Street Railroad Station in Oakland, just a bus ride away from North Beach. That's where my dad's friend lives, and from what Gary Daddy-o told us, his friend has a really cool apartment and I can hardly wait to see what it looks like. I'm guessing I'll have my own room and I think Ray will, too.

We got in around 7:30 in the morning but we've been twiddling our thumbs for a while, waiting for Gary Daddy-o. I try not to remind myself that if Nell-mom and my dad were still together, we'd be in New York and none of this would be happening.

We'd probably be going to Rockefeller Center this morning to see the big tree and the skaters. The streets around there smell of roasted chestnuts, which remind me of me of butter and vanilla mixed together, but never taste as good as they smell. Gary Daddy-o's usually pretty busy this time of year, playing at nightclubs and parties. We always get clementines and blood oranges, plus a little chocolate for dessert. Or would, if we didn't live apart.

The clock says it's half-past nine, but I'm all turned around because California is three hours behind New York. So, nine-thirty a.m. here is twelve thirty there, and who knows what that means if you want lunch and all you can find is breakfast? Not that I want to spend money on a restaurant, though the smell of bacon and eggs is everywhere and I think you'd have to be deaf not to hear my stomach growling.

The station's cool, though not as cool as the New York stations, but it's definitely old-time architecture by the way everything looks. I should be tired because I didn't get much sleep on the train, even though we had a sleeper car. I was just too excited.

It's starting to feel like we've been here forever and I'm getting kind of worried Gary Daddy-o won't show. "Do you think he overslept?" I ask Ray, who's looking around the room and trying to pretend he isn't, at the same time.

"What'll we do?" I say.

"Hold on a second. Let's think about this," Ray says, and we sit down on some worn-looking chairs near the door. We have two small suitcases, since Nell-mom always says you need to travel light. She means you have to keep moving, and I have to say I'm right there with her because lugging your suitcase around everywhere you go is a stinky idea, especially when it's early and you can barely walk yourself.

Ray and I sit a while in silence, and I can tell my brother doesn't have a clue what we should do. The thing about Ray is he'll always say stuff like, "Let's think about this," and then kind of stare off into space. He wants *you* to believe he's *thinking*, even if he doesn't do it very much.

The good news, if there is any, is that we have Gary Daddy-o's address. The not-as-good news is that we need to get a bus there and we have no idea what bus number to take. Plus, I don't know if the place he's staying has a telephone, let alone what number we'd call. Besides, if my dad's on his way, we could wind up at his place and he'd be here looking for us. It's probably better to just stay and wait a little longer, even though it's the last thing you want when you've been traveling.

"Shoeshine, miss?"

I turn my head just slightly to see two guys and a chick. They all look about sixteen. One of the guys has a blue T-shirt and the other has a purple one. The chick's in a black leather jacket and they're all in jeans. The guy in the blue shirt sprays some goop on my shoe and the other guy sprays the stuff on Ray's.

"Where you from?" says the chick.

I'm so surprised all I can say is, "Where YOU from?"

"L. A.," she says with a wink, like it's a joke between us. "D'you come from Chicago?"

I can tell she's trying to figure me out by finding out where I come from—but I'm not going to tell her that. I shrug instead, while the guy who sprayed my shoes pulls out a little rag and wipes them. The other guy wipes Ray's shoes a second later.

"That'll be seven dollars," the chick says.

I say, "*What*?"

"You heard me, darlin," she says, and I notice a little scar on the side of her forehead and another on the edge of her chin. She has striking green eyes, and long, dark hair like mine, only hers reaches almost to her knees.

"We don't even have three dollars," I say.

"Sure you do," she replies, like we're talking about the weather. "You've got those nice suitcases, and I bet they're worth seven apiece at least."

I laugh. "We don't have anything."

"How 'bout five? I mean just five bucks, come on!"

Is she asking because they really need the money, or because they're conning us? Probably both. And because I want to be a poet, I guess, I always feel like when I get into something like this, there's part of me that sees what's happening as sort of a story. This one feels like *The Snow Queen* with the Little Robber Girl, only this chick is the Big Robber Girl, or at least bigger than the little one.

"Come on," the chick says. "Five dollars won't kill ya, and it's for a good cause."

"What cause?" I ask. I know I shouldn't be talking to her, but can't help myself. I wish I could ask her where she got her scars, but then she'd probably tell me and that would make things worse, somehow. More entangled.

"Never mind," says Ray, and I think, *finally! Where were you, asleep?*

"Miss," he continues, "We didn't ask you to shine our shoes. And sorry, but—we really don't have any money."

She turns to look at him and smiles, slow and easy. "You know, I hear that all the time. But you know what?" She doesn't wait for us to answer. "People always do, somehow. It's a funny thing."

Her smile is like something you might see in a cartoon, with the corners of her mouth nearly touching her ears. What I'm trying to say is she's really pretty, except when she smiles because her smile is just pretend and has nothing to do with what she's thinking—there's a lot of ugly in that smile. Then I notice the guys with her have really big arms, like they've been working out forever.

"Those are really sweet little suitcases."

"No they're not," I say.

"We shined your shoes, little girl. And one way or another you're going to pay for it—"

"I'm not little—"

"You look little," the chick says. "What are you, ten?"

"No."

"Nine?"

"If I was nine, you'd be even creepier than you already are," I say, and suddenly the chick's smile disappears like I wiped it with the rag her friends were using.

"Don't you talk to me—"

"You're the one who started talking."

She doesn't reply this time, but lunges at my suitcase. She pulls so hard I almost let go and then one of the guys goes behind me and the other lunges at Ray, who socks him square in the mouth.

"*Hey!*" the chick yells, and then suddenly a guy about halfway across the room looks over at us.

"What's going *on*?" he calls out, and the chick lets go of my suitcase. The guys pull away too, and start running off, with the chick turning around quickly and scampering after them. I watch them go and feel my breath slowing down. It's been a million miles an hour as soon as I saw them.

"Everything okay?" the man asks, coming toward us. He's in a light-brown jacket and hat and what you call a goat-tee beard. I think that's because it's the same as goats wear.

"Looks like those kids were trying to rob you."

Ray puts up his hand. "We're okay now, thanks!" he says, and then says, "I hope," under his breath. The man tips his hat and walks off again, which is just as well since there's nothing going on at this point. I look at Ray, hoping he'll say something soothing like you'd want a big brother to say. Instead, he's glaring at me like everything that happened just now is my fault.

"You had to talk to her?"

"What else was I supposed to do?" I ask.

"Shut up and walk away? Do you ever consider that?"

"Where was I going to walk to? And you were just parked there like a zombie."

"I was thinking—"

"Like that ever gets us anywhere—"

"She *took* us, Ruby. They all did."

I look around the room, noticing the man with the goat beard is gone. And something makes me wonder if he was in on the whole thing, too, though I'll never be able to prove it.

"We've still got our suitcases," I say.

"They didn't want our suitcases."

"Yes, they *did*—"

Ray shakes his head, but doesn't say anything.

"What?" I say to him. "What else did they want?"

"Where's your satch?" he asks.

"*What?*"

He shakes his head again. "Yeah."

I look at Ray and my heart starts pumping just like it did a few minutes ago—only worse. Ray is staring at my arm, and I look down, seeing the empty space where the black strap for my bag is supposed to be.

Half bag, half purse, half satchel with sort of a buttery feel to it. I think it's imitation leather instead of real, with all these random pockets I can stash things in. Chaz gave it to me as an early Christmas present and I've been attached to it ever since. Keys, pens, notebook—my new notebook that I've written thirteen poems in already. A powder compact Sophie gave me with a mirror; a comb, brush, a red pencil because I like colored pencils, a black beret, and—

And.

Gary Daddy-o's address, of course. And.

And.

No. *No.*

My wallet.

4

BUSING IT

ROBBER CHICK AND her friends are long gone, but that doesn't stop me from running after them, even though I have no idea where they went. I'm reaching for the outside door when Ray grabs my arm.

"Ruby—"

"They stole our money!" I yell. "They have our dad's address—"

Ray puts up his hands like he always does when he's trying to calm things down. A few people are staring at us, but I don't care.

"I have his address," Ray says. "I've had it for a while. I know where we can find him—"

"We have no idea how to get there, and we have no money—"

"I have a little," says Ray. "Let me ask someone how to get a bus and we'll go."

I sit on the suitcase while Ray walks over to the ticket booth. I'm holding on to Ray's suitcase at the same time. I'm furious I even talked to that chick and that we didn't just smack those suitcases at them and run. I don't want to get on a bus and miss Gary Daddy-o if he's coming here, but on the other hand, I'm not exactly comfortable sitting around this station anymore.

If Gary Daddy-o does walk in here and tries to find us, he'll probably head home anyway, if we're not around. I'm so mad at him right now I don't even care what he does. I'm tired and hungry and I want a shower. The only good thing I can say about San Francisco is that it's a lot warmer than New York.

Ray comes back with a bus map, and we pick up our suitcases and walk outside. It's foggy enough to make me squint as we're walking and though I want to take in all the sights around me, I find myself trudging along, looking down at my shoes. Ray has to say, "Heads up!" a few times to stop me from bumping into something.

"What's the matter with you?" he asks.

"Tired," I say. "It's not every day you ride all across the country and someone robs you blind when you get off the train."

"Yeah, well." Ray says that a lot and I hate it. "We'll get something to eat soon."

I hope so. The bus driver opens the door and smiles, which is odd, but then I remember we're in California and

Sophie once told me people smile a lot more out there. I mean here, since this is where we are at the moment.

"Where you goin'?" the driver asks.

"North Beach," Ray says.

"You mean where the Beats are?" says the driver.

Ray nods, and we both kind of brace ourselves for what the driver may say next. Some people don't like Beats, even if they don't know any, but this driver just nods and smiles, so it looks like he doesn't have a problem with us.

Ray pays for our tickets and the bus door closes behind us. We sit close to the front so we don't miss anything. It's a lot easier to look out the window when someone else is carting you around than when you're walking with a suitcase, which I've got right under my knees. I could put it on a shelf above us, but I'm not letting go of anything after losing my bag. Ray's suitcase is under his knees, too, and he says his wallet is still inside his pocket, which is the luckiest part of the morning right now.

The train station has arches that make it look like pictures of buildings in Spain. Chaz showed me a couple before we left for California and said I might see a lot of those. Besides the train station, though, the buildings around here seem regular, like the row houses in New York but with lighter colors. It looks a little run down until we cross a bridge to San Francisco. Once we're over the bridge, it seems sunnier and brighter. People are walking around, and it looks like a ton of them are Christmas shopping. The buildings have more colors, like Nell-mom's pastels—pink, yellow, green, and brown. It still seems weird to see people in light jackets without hats and gloves. I stuffed mine in my coat pocket and Ray and I both took our coats off as soon as we got on the bus.

I start thinking about whether or not Gary Daddy-o will have a Christmas tree, but something tells me he won't. If he was still with Maddie in D. C., I know they'd have one, but since he's by himself here, he's probably letting it slide and I don't even know if he's in the mood for a holiday.

When we all lived on Perry Street in Greenwich Village, he and Nell-mom would bring home a tree and we'd all stay up way past midnight decorating it with popcorn and cranberries. Nell-mom said lights weren't all that cool since they're so *artificial.* We did have a couple of different ornaments we collected over the years from friends and stuff, and now and again, Nell-mom would make one and those were the best of all.

The last Christmas we were all together was a year ago and Nell-mom said we should each make three things for everyone else in the family and make it a surprise, so you wrapped up your presents in your room. I made up poems for everyone and also made a beaded necklace for my mom. I gave Gary Daddy-o a paperweight and found a record of Elvis singing "Jailhouse Rock" for my brother.

I also got Ray, Nell-mom and Gary Daddy-o each a pack of Juicy Fruit gum, which was funny because they all got packs for me, too, so I had three of them.

I got a bunch of cool stuff that year, but my favorite was a Sputnik necklace from Gary Daddy-o. Everybody was talking about Sputnik last year, because it was this weird-looking satellite launched into space by the Russians. They were trying to win the space race, and nobody thought they could, but everyone wanted a Sputnik necklace anyway. I wore that necklace every day for months and then at a street fair, there were tons of people milling around and somehow or other, I lost it.

I can't ask my dad to get me another one this year— for one thing, they're pretty expensive. We're going to need all the money we have just to get a Christmas tree, but maybe Gary Daddy-o and Ray can get some money playing on the street or Gary Daddy-o can juggle somewhere.

I think about what the chicklet who stole my wallet is doing right now. I imagine her going into a store and buying some kind of leotard or eating a fancy dinner. I know I need to stop thinking about her, but I can't.

Ray, meanwhile, is asking the bus driver how to find our dad's address. The driver tells him, and Ray tells me to write it down, but of course my pencil is in my satchel, and who knows where that is right now.

"I've got a pen," the driver says, reaching into his pocket and handing it to Ray, who hands it to me with the piece of paper that has the address: 114 Varennes Street, San Francisco. The driver tells us to walk up Columbus toward Grant Avenue and curve to the right a little to get onto Grant. Then we're supposed to turn right onto Green Street and then walk a little ways to

Varennes and turn left. Seems pretty easy, Ray says, and thanks the driver.

We stop at a light and I look at Ray. It seems like he's growing up faster these days, but I don't know if that's really true or if he's been doing it for a while and I just haven't noticed. He seems a little sadder than he used to be, too. I mean he's still messy and throws his clothes everywhere. But otherwise, he seems to have gotten quieter than he used to be. He also seems to want to hang out more with his girl Jo-Jo and doesn't have as many friends as he had when he was younger. Which is good, but not so good? I don't know.

"Mad at me?" I ask.

"No," he says, but he still isn't looking at me.

"You sure?"

"It wasn't your fault," he says.

"You said it was—"

"It wasn't."

We both look out the window for a while, not talking. I want to talk about Gary Daddy-o, and at the same time it feels scary to talk, because I don't want to imagine things that may not be true—like him sitting in a bar somewhere, forgetting what day it is and trying not to fall off his stool.

"Rubes." Ray shakes my arm and points to the door. "This is where we get off."

There's only one other person on the bus, a guy in back who's snoring. I pick up the handle of my suitcase and pull it toward me as I stand. Ray gets off first and when I step off the bus and look up, I can hardly believe my eyes. Big gold lettering curves in a semi-circle just ahead of us: Inner Pages—with a windowful of books displayed underneath. I can't believe this is what I'm looking at after all this time.

Suddenly all the tired and hungry I was carrying vanishes and all I want to do is go inside. Gary Daddy-o once took me to a movie where a man was walking in the desert for days and his tongue was hanging out of his mouth and he was dying of thirst and then out of the blue he sees a little pond full of water with palm trees all around and runs like the devil to jump inside. He falls down and starts licking at the water and then starts coughing, because it's what you call a mirage, which means the man is imagining it and all he's licking is sand.

This is no mirage. All I have to do is walk seven steps to open the door and I'll be inside the most famous bookstore in the world, at least the Beat world. I look at Ray and he's looking at the window, too. But then he turns to me.

"Ruby—"

"Don't—"

"We've got to find Gary Daddy-o," he says, and I know he's right, but I'm not sure I can just turn around and pretend I'm not here right now. I can't help but think about who is in there and if they're an author or a poet and whether people are listening to them read or not. When a man opens the door, I want to rush inside behind him—and at the same time, I'm so tired and I want to lie down so badly I can hardly think straight.

I look at the man walking into the bookstore and force myself to look away. I want to be myself when I walk into this place. I don't want to be dragging a suitcase and worried about where my dad may be. Inner Pages deserves my full attention.

I turn to Ray.

"Let's get home and come back later?"

He nods and says we have to head up Columbus Avenue toward Broadway. We start walking and I make a pact with myself that every day I'm here I'm walking to that bookstore and I'm going to read all the books I've heard about—including the new one by Lawrence Ferlinghetti called *A Coney Island of the Mind*. I have a feeling all the Beat poets I ever heard of stop by there. Just being around them, maybe talking to them or at least going to their readings, will help me make my own poetry better. That's why Nell-mom visits galleries—to see how other painters think.

We turn onto Grant Avenue and go uphill, which isn't a lot of fun when you're dragging suitcases. Luckily it doesn't take too long to get to Green Street and we turn right. We see Varennes pretty soon and turn left and there's 114, near the corner. It looks like it's three stories and Ray says Gary Daddy'o's place is on the second floor. There's ironwork around the door and I don't see a bell, so we knock and knock again, but there's no answer. I start pounding on the door and suddenly a man with glasses opens the door. "Whatcha want?" he asks.

Ray tells him we're looking for our dad in apartment 2A. He lets us in and we walk up the stairs.

I'm thinking Gary Daddy-o is at the railroad station and it'll be hours until we get in, and when Ray knocks on the door, no one answers.

I feel like I want to scream, but when Ray turns the doorknob, miraculously, the door opens. It's kind of dark inside, but we can sort of make out a couch and a blue-green rug that covers most of what must be the living room. There's a kitchen and hallway off to the left but I see a dark shape on the floor in front of the couch and my heart skips a beat.

I know without knowing it's Gary Daddy-o, still as a rock on the carpeted floor with a blanket over his head. No sound is coming from underneath the blanket and there's no sound in the apartment, either. In fact, I've never seen Gary Daddy-o like this and I doubt Ray has, either. I want to go over and shake him, but I'm also kind of scared. Because if I do shake him and nothing happens…

…what then?

Is he asleep? Why would he be sleeping on the floor?

I realize I've been clutching my suitcase since I walked in here and put it down, rubbing my hand.

What's going on with you, Gary Daddy-o?

Are you alive? Dead?

I have no idea.

5

WASHINGTON SQUARE DANCE

"WHAT'S GOING ON?" Someone is screaming and I realize it's me. My voice is hoarse and broken and I can't make it stop. "What's the matter with him?"

"Ruby—"

Ray gives up on trying to stop me and touches Gary Daddy-o's shoulder instead. He opens his eyes, or at least one eye, and peers at us.

"What's up?" he says, like we've all been hanging around together for the past forty years.

"What happened?" I say, trying to cool down but not quite getting there.

Gary Daddy-o pulls himself up on his elbow and stares at me.

"Ruby?"

"Who else?" I say, trying as hard as I can to take it easy.

"I was supposed to pick you up this morning?"

"Yeah," I tell him. "What happened?"

"I'm sorry, baby," he says, and just his saying that makes me feel like crying. I hold my breath instead.

"I thought it was tomorrow," Gary Daddy-o says.

I look at him, speechless, and Ray pipes up before either of us can say another word.

"It's okay, Pops. We're here."

Ray calls our dad "Pops" these days. I don't think Gary Daddy-o likes it, but we're all kind of used to it by now.

"I'm sorry," Gary Daddy-o says.

"Why were you on the floor?"

"I didn't want to mess up the couch," he answers. "Came in late and just thought I'd sit up for a while, you know. I must have conked out."

That's when I notice the stubble all over Gary Daddy-o's face and the way his shirt is half unbuttoned. There's a smell in the air, too—a little like the bums in the Village at home, who smell like they've been pickled in some sort of vinegar and haven't had a bath in a long, long time. I look at Ray, who's on the other side of Gary Daddy-o, and he's wrinkling his nose, too.

"You want to take a shower?" I ask.

"Don't you?" he says, and for the first time since I walked in the door, my dad sits all the way up and faces me.

"I'll take one right after," I tell him, "but I want you to have one first."

He starts to argue but I stop him by holding my

nose. "*Please?* You smell really weird right now."

He looks at me and I can tell I hurt him a little. At the same time, I can't stand the thought of him being so stinky and I need him to know that.

He rubs his eyes for a second. "Okay."

Without missing a beat, Ray puts his hand out and hooks it under Gary Daddy-o's arm. I do the same thing and we help him up, and while part of me is waiting for him to stop us, he doesn't.

"Where's the bathroom?" Ray asks.

Gary Daddy-o points us in the right direction and then pulls away. "I'm fine. Just do me a favor and call your mom," he says, and I know he's saying that because Nell-mom worries more about us than she did when my parents were together. Whatever he may do that drives you crazy, my dad is a really nice guy.

He turns away and half walks, half shuffles into the hall. I follow him, trying to make sure he's all right while pretending I'm just looking at the furniture. He walks into one of the rooms at the end of the hall and closes the door. After a couple minutes, I hear the sound of the shower being turned on and go back to the living room. There's a phone next to the couch and I pick it up and call my mother.

"Hello?" Nell-mom chirps, like she does when she's trying to be extra cheery. I chirp right back, saying, "Hi!" Then I tell her, "Ray and I are with Gary Daddy-o."

"Thank God!" she says, which tells me my dad was right about the worrying.

"Everything's fine," I tell her.

"You sure?" she asks.

Why do people always say that when you tell them you're fine? Or is it only mothers? What happens when you become a mom—do you turn into a worry machine?

"Ruby?"

I need to stop having this conversation. "Want to say hi to Ray?"

"Uh, sure!" she says, and I hand over the phone so Ray can do the talking. Sun is pouring through the living room window and I start to understand, for the first time, that Ray and I are really in California. I let out my breath and sit down.

"Love you, Mom," Ray says into the phone. He looks at me to see if I want to talk to Nell-mom again. I shake my head, so he says goodbye.

"Is there anything to eat in this place?" I ask, and Ray looks straight at me like I'm some kind of fairy godmother.

"I have no idea," he says, and the next thing I know we're both laughing like hyenas, so hard I double over and Ray opens his mouth so I can see all his teeth and it's a while before we can stop. We walk into the kitchen, which is bright with white cabinets everywhere, and a bowl of fruit on the counter. I make a beeline for it, but when I pick up some grapes I can see they're moldy and throw them back down.

Meanwhile, Ray is opening the refrigerator and pulls out some milk. He opens the bottle and smells it, making a face. "Sour," he says, and puts it down. I notice a box of Cheerios on the other side of the counter and pick it up. "I think we can have this," I say, "even without the milk."

"He's got orange juice," Ray says, leaning into the refrigerator. "We can pour it on the cereal."

"No thanks," I say, "I'll have it dry. But I'll drink some of that juice right now."

Ray finds some glasses and pours some juice out for us. I find two bowls and watch him pour juice on his cereal. If I wasn't so hungry I'd throw up, but instead I'm reaching into my bowl and pulling out a couple of Cheerios at a time, trying to eat them S-L-O-W-L-Y. If I had milk I'd go digging around for sugar and eat every bit of that bowl except the bowl part.

Ray digs into his cereal and I can't help ribbing him. "How can anyone eat Cheerios and orange juice?"

"That's the best part." I look up to see Gary Daddy-o in the doorway. He's in a faded black shirt and jeans and looks amazingly awake and smiley. He smells better, too—like the after-shave lotion Old Spice that he started wearing when he lived with Maddie. "You really ought to try some OJ on your cereal," he says.

"No, thanks," I say.

Gary Daddy-o turns to Ray. "You up for playing somewhere a little later?"

"Sure," says Ray. "You have a gig or something?"

"Just on the street," Gary Daddy-o says. "But we can make some good money."

"Okay," says Ray.

We both know what Gary Daddy-o's telling us. We're going to have to do some street theater if we want groceries. Gary Daddy-o will juggle, Ray will play sax and I can either recite some poetry or dance. It's a pretty good idea because there isn't much in the refrigerator and I have a feeling more than grapes are rotting. The only thing is, Ray didn't bring his saxophone.

"I've got three saxophones here," Gary Daddy-o says as if he's reading my mind. "Cat who's on tour right now plays them."

"Is there an alto?" Ray asks.

"Yep! Plus baritone and soprano."

"Sounds good, Pops," Ray says, and Gary Daddy-o says he'll shave and then we can each have a shower.

He walks down the hall and I shake some more cereal into my bowl. Ray does, too, and we both drink up the orange juice double quick. By the time Gary Daddy-o gets out of the bathroom, I'm finished with breakfast and trying to figure out how old the eggs in the fridge might be.

"We'll get some new stuff later," Gary Daddy-o tells me. "Why don't you get cleaned up, honey, and I'll take your stuff to your room."

I nod and smile, thinking maybe it'll all work out and I was worried for nothing. Gary Daddy-o looks great and the place he found is amazing. It's bigger than it looked at first and a lot airier, with two bedrooms and a foldout couch for Ray. I tell him we can switch off on the bedroom but he says it's only a couple weeks and he likes foldouts, anyway.

I change into jeans and the one blue sweater I have, which is royal blue, Gary Daddy-o's favorite color. He tells me I need more blue stuff, but I tell him most of what I've always had is black. He shakes his head and laughs. "Course you do. My Beat girl."

I tell him look who's talking, since most of what he and Ray wear is black, too, except some blue jeans now and then. He turns away to look for something, and I'm guessing it's his juggling balls, so I ask if I can help. He says no and goes into his room, and in about two minutes he comes out again with a pair of bongos.

"What?" I say. "Don't tell me you're playing those."

"Your old man taught himself," he tells me. "That big old bass is too big to lug around on the street."

I'm guessing if Gary Daddy-o's playing bongos now, he's playing pretty good, because as long as I've known him he's been good at music. It might be the one thing he loves more than anything else, including my mom or anyone else he's ever been with. I'm not sure if that's true for Ray, but I think it might be, and I know how they feel, kinda-sorta. I like writing almost as much, especially poem writing, because whatever I'm doing, no matter what it is, I'm always thinking if I can turn it into a poem.

"You ready?" Gary Daddy-o asks, and Ray and I both say, "Sure!" at the same time, which makes us laugh. Ray pulls out the alto sax from its case and practices on it a while before we go. Gary Daddy-o plays bongos along with him and I try to think up some poems I can say by heart. By the time we go out, I'm thinking of us like traveling musicians in the Middle Ages. I think they called them troubadours.

The street's so alive, it could be singing. Ladies in cloth driving coats and heels carry shopping bags with presents they might have saved for all year. A juggler on the corner tips his hat to us, and I tip an imaginary hat right back. Two businessmen in hats walk by yakking, and a little girl in a green dress and matching jacket begs her father for a doll. The sky is the bluest I've ever seen it—so yeah, no wonder my dad wanted to be here. It's like Greenwich Village, but there's ocean all around and flowers everywhere. It's the most beautiful city I've ever seen.

I don't know where we are, exactly, but Gary Daddy-o leads us over toward Filbert Street. We turn left and go down to Stockton and there's a park on the left. "Welcome to Washington Square Park," Gary Daddy-o says with a smile. "Number Two."

"No kidding!" Ray says, and we both smile. "No wonder you live here," I say, and that makes Gary Daddy-o smile too, since there's a Washington Square Park just a few blocks from our place in New York.

We walk around a bit so Gary Daddy-o can find just the right spot, where there are enough people passing by to make it worth our while. Once we find it, Ray opens his saxophone case and picks up his instrument. Gary Daddy-o kneels on the ground and starts playing bongos.

I put the open case in front of us and let them play a while, waiting to see if they'll draw a crowd. I wish I had my notebook, because I'm drawing a blank about what I've written, and besides that, I'm feeling kind of shy. I love writing poetry, but I don't perform it much. I'd like to, but the street is hard. You have to be really good here or you could get pelted. And if you think the grapes were rotten in our dad's apartment, you should see what they throw in the street.

I decide to try dancing instead. It's easy to move around to the music, and it might be hard to hear me talking over the sax and everything else that's going on. Nell-mom taught me some free-style moves this year when she had musicians play at some of her gallery shows. Nobody ran out screaming, so I figure it was at least passable—and the best part of dancing is you don't have to talk to anyone.

I start dancing around, finding the beat so I move in rhythm to it. People are starting to gather and when the first song ends, they applaud.

We do five, seven, ten songs, and by then I am exhausted, but when I look at Gary Daddy-o and Ray, they look like they are just getting started. "Shall we go for a few more?" Gary Daddy-o asks, and Ray nods, but I say I want to sit the next few out.

"Don't you want a Christmas tree?" Gary Daddy-o asks, and of course I do. He winks at me and I guess that means I have to keep going for a while. I keep dancing in and out of the spaces between people and even get a few to dance with me. Gary Daddy-o steps up his game and Ray riffs up and down the scale on his saxophone. I'm pretty sure we must have played at least an hour or more before we stop. Not enough money as we wanted, Gary Daddy-o says, but it'll do for now.

Ray puts the coins into a hollow section at the bottom of the saxophone case. There's at least a few dollar bills, so there should be enough for some eats. Once Ray packs up, Gary Daddy-o leans over and gives me a hug. It's the first time we hugged in a long time, and I think he's about to pick me up like I was a little kid. I give him a look and he stops, but I almost wish he had.

We walk back to the apartment and put everything away before we go shopping. Gary Daddy-o seems to know everyone at the grocery store, which is just a few blocks away from where we're staying. There's a tall woman with dark hair swept up in a French twist, who jokes with him and winks at us. A bald man in glasses behind the counter asks our names and tells us our dad is his best pal.

Another box of Cheerios, milk, bananas, apples, oranges, spaghetti, sauce and tuna cans fill up our cart pretty quickly. Ray finds bread, peanut butter, and marmalade (his favorite), and I find pancake mix, which Garry Daddy-o says I can have. We don't have enough for much else, but some chicken legs are on sale, so we get those.

I haven't seen this much food in days and I'm practically floating. I tell Gary Daddy-o I want to stay in San Francisco forever and he says yeah, he knows. "It's the most beautiful city in the whole country."

"I'd say the world," I tell him, and Ray agrees. We walk home with three bags of groceries and I ask if I can sit down for a few minutes before we put them away. Gary Daddy-o says he'll do it and I sit on the couch, looking out the window at the sky.

The next thing I know, I'm in bed with the covers pulled up around me. I don't even know how long I've been asleep.

6

SORROW ENDS HERE

IT TAKES ABOUT seven minutes to walk to Inner Pages, but if you run, you can probably get there in half the time. Ray and Gary Daddy-o were still sleeping, and the kitchen clock said 10:30, so believe it or not, I was probably asleep since dinner time the day before.

With only a couple weeks here I couldn't waste another second without going to the bookstore. I wolf down cereal and write a note (because you *always* write a note if you don't want parents blowing their jets, like Nell-mom says). I run so fast I can see people staring at me like I'm in trouble or something—but I don't care.

The sign at the door of Inner Pages says, "Sorrow Ends Here." I half expect it to be so noisy you can't hear yourself, but it's not so much loud as full of babble because everyone in here is talking at the same time.

I've got fifteen cents, which should buy me at least one book—but what to choose? I ask where the poetry section is and a man points downstairs. There's a sign over the stairs going upwards, saying, "How the mighty are fallen when they don't hold onto the handrails." I laugh out loud and a bunch of people look at me, smiling.

I trot downstairs and find a goldmine, with more Beat Generation books than I've ever seen in my life. There are books by all the Beat poets: Gregory Corso, Allen Ginsberg, Jack Kerouac, Denise Levertov, Kenneth Patchen. Lawrence Ferlinghetti's book *Coney Island of the Mind* and *Pictures of the Gone World* are here, too.

The poets are all different, but what I love about them all is how they don't care about whether they're rhyming or not like the old-fashioned poets. They have their own rhythms, like jazz, mostly, and they write free-form and from the gut, which is what Nell-mom says she tries to do with her painting. I want to check out the Levertov book because Nell-mom says you have to be twice as good as men when you're writing or painting, since getting poems published if you're not a man is nearly impossible.

I see a book of poems called *Here and Now* by Denise Levertov, but can't get to it because there's a woman on a ladder right in front of it. It looks like she's arranging books, and I don't want to mess with her. But while I'm staring up at her, wondering what to do, she looks down at me and says, "Hi."

"Hello," I reply. It's easier to hear what she's saying down here since there's a lot less people.

"Looking for something?"

"Just… looking," I say, feeling shy.

"If you need anything, let me know," the woman says. I look at her a little closer and can't help being a little surprised. She's old and crinkly, which wasn't what you'd expect in a place like Inner Pages. By old, I mean she has thick white hair, brushed back from her face, and lots of crinkles around her eyes, which are greenish-blue and really large. She's wearing a sleeveless vest that hangs down to her hips, and black leggings.

The woman's nose is so straight it reminds me of an Egyptian statue, and even though she's probably sixty or even older, her arms are tight and muscular and her posture's much better than mine ever was. And while part of me wants to slink off and disappear, part of me wants to keep talking and see exactly what book *she'd* choose if she could only have one. So that's what I ask.

"Really? Well. Let's see." Little lines darken in her forehead while she thinks about it.

"I want to read *Here and Now*," I say, "But I also want to read *Howl* and everything else in here. I've only got money for one, though."

"You can buy one and read the others here," the woman says. "Except I think some of the books aren't—I need to find out if we can sell them to kids."

"Well, I'm not exactly a kid," I say. "Pretty soon I'll be a teenager."

"How old are you?" she asks.

57

Jenna Zark

"Twelve. But I'll be thirteen in April."

"Yeah, I mean. We'd have to ask the owner."

"Well, is there anything I could read right now?" I ask.

She climbs down the ladder. "You know, Denise Levertov sent her poems to T. S. Eliot when she was twelve," she says, "and he liked them so much he wrote back to her. I think her first poem was published when she was seventeen."

"I want to start with her, then," I say, and the woman takes one of the Levertov books off the shelf and hands it to me. "My name is Ruth, by the way."

"I'm Ruby," I say. And before I know it, I've told her where I came from and how I'm visiting my dad and hope I can be a poet when I'm older. Except I don't want to be a poet if I'm not good at it, and Ruth says she understands. She moved here from New York a few years ago, so us both being New Yorkers is one thing we already have in common. Ruth has been working at the bookstore for about a year, not only selling books, but as an editor for the books they're publishing. I tell her (without being able to help myself) that's probably the coolest thing I've heard anybody say in forever. That makes her smile.

Besides being an editor, Ruth is a dancer. In fact, she was in a dance troupe in New York and would like to join one here, but is probably too old, she says. I kind of agree, but on the other hand, it seems unfair. "Maybe you can start your own troupe," I say, and she looks at me like I said something really interesting.

A few more people walk by us and say hello to Ruth, and she says hello back. A guy with glasses holding a

copy of *Howl* tells her she's got to come to Blabbermouth
Night at the Place on Thursday, since he's going to
be speaking. "I'll be sure to stay away," she says, and
they laugh. The guy looks down at me and asks if I'm
her granddaughter, which makes me blush. I've never
known a grandmother, and wouldn't mind having one,
but don't want Ruth to be embarrassed.

"She's a new friend, I hope," Ruth says, and I look
up at Ruth, wanting to smile and stay cool at the same
time. Smiling wins, though.

"Welcome," the man says, and puts out his hand
like he wants to shake mine. I take his and he tells
me his name is Nelson. "You tell her to come to
Blabbermouth Night, and come along," he says. Which
of course makes me ask what that means, and he says
it's a night at the Place Café where different people get
up in front of everyone and talk about whatever they
want. "Usually politics," he says.

Ruth says, "Don't let him talk you into it, Ruby.
Nelson can go on for hours."

"I'll see if I can get my dad to go," I say.

"That's the spirit," says Nelson, before he strolls away.

Ruth shakes her head, smiling, and watches Nelson
go before turning back to me. "Would you like to get
lunch, Ruby?" she asks. "I get a break in a little bit and
there's a place that's not too far from here. I think you
would like it."

"I, um, don't have any money—" I say.

"No matter," she says, "I have money, and it'd be great
to have some company." She says to go pay for my book

and she'll meet me upstairs. I know mostly you're not supposed to go out with a stranger, but meeting her at Inner Pages and seeing Nelson and all makes me feel like it's okay. Nell-mom always says to trust your hunches, and I think I'm pretty good about that, so I say yes.

"Okay, meet you in a minute," I say. While I'm waiting on line to buy my book, I look around at the store. There are so many books the shelves are sagging almost everywhere. All the signs are hand-lettered and there are tons of them. "A Kind of Library Where Books Are Sold," one reads, and another says, "Have a Seat and Read a Book."

Being here feels like being in the middle of Beat Heaven. It could be how the sun shines in through the windows or how it seems more like a church than a store. The babble I heard when I got here seems to have died down, and people mostly talk softly to each other. I never thought anywhere in the world would be more interesting than New York—but Inner Pages has it beat in hundreds of ways.

I buy the book with a penny to spare, which seems so funny I tell them to keep it. The lady behind the counter says no. "It's your lucky penny," she says. "For a lucky day."

I put the penny in my pocket and turn around to see Ruth at the door. By the time I reach her, she's opened the door and is holding it for me. I can see the Vesuvio Café right near us and I think we're going in there, but Ruth steers me up the block a ways, saying she hopes I like Italian food. I tell her my dad is Italian and I better like it. She laughs. She walks really fast and I have to hustle to keep up with her, especially while I'm trying to take in everything that's going on all over the street.

There are at least as many Beats in this town as there are in Greenwich Village. With Christmas coming, a lot of them are trying to sell paintings or books or even berets and turtlenecks. Tourists are all over the place here, too, but I don't have time to look in any store windows because Ruth is tugging my arm and bringing me inside the restaurant where she wants to eat lunch. It's called the U. S. Restaurant.

A couple is behind the counter and Ruth introduces them to me.

"Ruby, these are my friends Camilla and Joe."

Camilla waves and says, "Good morning, Ruby!" She has shortish dark hair, and is wearing glasses and an apron over a short-sleeved dress. There's a teeny bit of a curl right over her forehead. Joe has a mustache and his hair is partly black and party silver. He's got rolled-up sleeves and a black vest, and Ruth says lunch hour is starting in about fifteen minutes so it's a good thing we're in here now. The whole place reminds me a little of Rocco's back home, but it's a little more like a restaurant instead of a café.

Camilla tells us to order whatever we want. "Don't you worry, Ruby, we're gonna take good care of you."

I look at Ruth, who nods. We look over the menu and end up splitting a plate of ravioli, which I've only ever had once, and some meatballs and fresh parmesan cheese. They bring us water, but Ruth has coffee, too.

She asks me all about my life and I tell her the bits I mostly want her to know. She asks if she can read some of my poems, and I tell her my notebook was stolen on the way here.

"That's a shame," she says, frowning.

"I can try and remember some and write them down for you."

"Okay, Ruby," says Ruth. "It's a good idea to write them down again, anyway."

Joe brings me a little "honey tea," which is a really sweet kind of tea that he says is "on the house," so I don't have to pay for it. After about fifteen minutes, the restaurant starts to get more crowded and when Camilla brings our food, it seems like she and Joe are at the center of a party where practically everybody knows each other. "Buon Appetito" says Camilla, as she lowers our plates to the table.

The ravioli and meatballs are so delicious they make you want to eat a thousand of them, and it's all I can do to let Ruth have at least half the meal. We get some on-the-house fruit cocktail for dessert, and by then it's so busy we can barely get our bill paid, though it's really Ruth who's paying.

I thank her up and down, the way Nell-mom says you should, saying it was the kindest thing anyone's every done for me and all that, and she says stop and looks straight at me. "You can thank me, Ruby, but don't make it sound like I'm Master of the Universe or something."

"I don't mean—"

"It just sounds like it's phony. I know you don't mean to be."

"No, um. I don't."

I can feel my face getting as hot as if it were on fire. I want to explain that I've never had anybody like her be so cool about paying for me and it's not every day you get an old-fashioned Italian dinner because of a stranger you meet in a bookstore. I want to tell her my dad used to cook Italian for us sometimes and I always loved it. But I feel like anything I say at this point will sound phony, and just want to shrink into a hole somewhere.

I think Ruth can tell she made me feel bad, because she puts her hand on my shoulder and says, "It's okay, Ruby. It's not a big deal. I guess I don't do that well with compliments." I tell her I know what she means because I don't do well with them, either. She nods, and I start to feel a little better.

We keep walking, and Ruth starts talking about the neighborhood. It was mostly settled by Italians, and now there's lots of Beats here since the rent is cheap. With the bookstore and all, it's a great place to be if you're an artist.

"What you need to do if you go somewhere and you're a writer, is look at everything. And then like the painters say, if you can, see it in your own light," she says. "Like an artist would."

I look up at her, wondering what she's trying to tell me here.

"That means close your eyes a bit—not all the way,

but just a little, Ruby, and try to see it your own way. Maybe you see what it looked like before we all got here, like fifty, sixty years ago. Or longer! Talk to people like Camilla and Joe and find out about the streets you're walking on. There's always more story than what you see in front of you—not that you shouldn't write about what's in front of you, because that's important, too."

I want to tell her I will, but I'm not sure how to find people besides Camilla and Joe, who really know the neighborhood. As if she knows what I'm thinking, Ruth says to ask the bookstore owner, who everyone calls Mr. Z.

"Isn't he really busy?" I ask.

"Not for one of his employees."

"Huh?"

"We can ask if he'll give you a job, you know? Would you like that?"

My heart speeds up like a racecar and I stop in the middle of the street to look at her.

"Really?"

"Well, let's at least cross the street—"

"I'm supposed to be here visiting my dad," I say, "and I'm leaving after New Year's—"

"I'm just talking a few hours a day for the Christmas rush," Ruth says. "We pay cash, so you'd get your money pretty quickly. But it's okay if you're not interested."

"I'm INTERESTED!" I shout, and then want to kick myself for being such a jerk.

"All righty then," Ruth says, laughing, and I pull open the door and watch her step inside. I'm about to follow her when I bump into Ray, who's standing just inside the bookstore. I look up at him.

"What are *you* doing here?"

"I saw your note," he says.

"Who's this?" Ruth asks, and I introduce her to my brother. She asks him if he knows his sister is a poet, and he says sure, but instead of being friendly like he always is, Ray turns back to me with a worried expression.

"Gotta ask you to come home now," he says.

"What?"

"We've got to stick around, you know?" he says, and I can tell he wants to say more, but doesn't feel like he can.

"What's the matter?"

"Nothing, Ruby," he says. "I'm sorry to interrupt, and you can come back later. But right now, it's kind of… Anyway. You've got to come home."

7

GETTING IN

THE DOOR TO Gary Daddy-o's room is locked and it's scary quiet in there. Ray says he was banging on the door for half an hour before he came and got me. I'm surprised because Ray doesn't like to bang on anything, even a drum.

"Did you try the window?" I ask.

"We're on the second floor."

"Isn't there a fire escape?"

Ray has no idea. I turn and run out of the apartment with him at my heels. There's no fire escape in front, so I run to the corner and go a little ways until I see an alley behind the building. It takes a few minutes to find Gary Daddy-o's window, but once I do, I can see there's no fire escape. Instead, I see a black iron ladder that looks like you'd need to be a trapeze artist to climb it. Ray and I look up and it appears there are little balconies outside what seem to be the bedroom windows of this place. I look at Ray and he reads my mind instantly. "No."

"I can do it—"

"I don't want you to do it—"

"Let me try."

"I'll try—"

"Your feet are too big for this ladder. You'll slip—"

"You go first and I'll go right behind you. I'm not letting you go up there alone."

The main way to get brothers to go along is to throw ideas at them. Ray usually takes the bait like a fish, and I bet any other boy does, too. If you make something into a problem and start solving it, they have to jump in there with you. I know this from years of experience.

"Rubes! Go slowly."

"I get it," I say, turning to grab hold of the ladder. It's definitely iron, and hard as a rock. I step up onto the first rung, thinking the second floor just can't be that high, right? But the farther up I go, the higher it feels. Ray's practically crawling up my legs so I stop and tell him to hang back.

I step up again and keep going, willing myself not to look down. It's not all that warm out, but the sun's pretty bright and I can feel myself starting to sweat as I'm climbing. "Almost there!" says Ray.

Yeah, right, I think, but what happens when we get there? And what if someone comes by and sees us? It's not against the law, I guess, to climb up the side of a building, but I sure don't want someone to think we're trying to steal something. Luckily, we're on the back side of the house, in an alley, and I don't think it's likely anyone else is going to be around.

All of a sudden I slip, my left foot sliding from under me. It happens so fast I can barely think about how to stop myself, but reach out and grab the railing. The leaves of a tree in front of the house go sideways for a second or two before turning right side up again.

"Careful!" Ray yells, like I nearly killed myself on purpose.

I let out my breath, slowly. "What do you think I'm doing?"

"Rubes—"

"Be cool, Ray. I'm fine."

One, two, three, four. Eight more steps and I'm at the balcony, peering inside the window. Ray's a little behind me and I inch up close to the pane, trying to see through the curtains to be sure Gary Daddy-o's in there. All I can make out are shapes and shadows, so if this isn't where Gary Daddy-o's sleeping, I'm going to be in trouble.

I tap on the window, once, twice, and tap again. Nothing.

Ray edges toward me. "Lemme see if I can open it," he says, and I scooch over a bit to let him get closer. He jiggles the window as it rattles, but we still have no luck. I tap a few more times and then Ray starts jiggling again and wonder of wonders, the window starts to move. Slowly, Ray gets it up enough to curl his fingers around the bottom and lift. The window gets high enough so a very skinny person could slip through if she had to. That's going to have to be me, since the window doesn't seem to want to be lifted any further.

I slip my head inside, sideways, and see Gary Daddy-o is in bed, snoring lightly. There's a small bookcase on the wall underneath the window, and if I can just get past it, I should be able to get into the room. I decide to go headfirst, lowering my hands and arms to the floor. That's what our cat Solange does when she wants to get in somewhere. If her head can make it, she figures the rest of her can, too.

I can hear Ray breathing behind me as I slide toward the bookcase.

"Uh oh! What's going on here?" A woman's voice floats upward, startling me into slipping past the bookcase and falling onto the floor with my hands stretched out in front of me. Books crash all around the room.

"Whaaa?" Gary Daddy-o calls out as he opens his eyes.

"We're not burglars," Ray calls down to the woman below. "We're locked out—"

"Everything all right?" a man says. I'm guessing there's a couple on the street looking up at us.

"You bet! We live here," says Ray.

"My, my," the woman says. "Shall we ask the police for help?"

"We don't need any help," Ray tells her.

"And if we did, it wouldn't be from the police," I say, but I don't think anyone hears me.

Meanwhile, Gary Daddy-o is staring straight at me and then, somehow closes his eyes again. I don't understand how anyone could do this, but the next thing I know he's lying back down and almost sound asleep. I have no choice but to yell at him at the top of my lungs.

"Daddy-o! Wake up!"

He opens an eye and looks at me again. "Shhh."

"We're in trouble!" I say. "A couple downstairs thinks we're breaking in and they want to call the cops! Hurry!"

It's hard getting my father to hurry on the best of days, but right now if he was in a race with a turtle, I'm positive he'd lose. He does manage to sit up, and I can see he's wearing a white undershirt and boxer shorts. Meanwhile Ray keeps talking to the couple outside.

"I wouldn't worry about it. Let me see if we can get my dad to come downstairs."

"Take your time," the woman says. "We're not going anywhere. Just out for a little walk, is all." Her voice sounds trembly and creaky, and the man sounds a little stronger. I look outside and see an old lady with white hair in braids around her head, holding on to a younger man in a newsboy cap and jacket who seems like he could be her son. Everything about the woman seems a little creaky, but she doesn't look mean or angry. She's wearing a burgundy-colored coat and shoes the size of Cleveland. Her son has pretty big shoes on, too.

"Hold on," I say, and turn back to Gary Daddy-o again. His eyes are closing and he's sinking backwards.

"No!" I run over to the bed, practically jumping on him. "You've got to come down right now, or we'll all be in trouble."

He looks at me with one eye nearly closed and the other open. "What are you doing, Ruby?"

"I climbed up all the stairs on the back of this building to be sure you're okay."

"Every single step?" Gary Daddy-o asked, his eyes widening. I nodded.

"No kidding?" he says, and then says, "Look at you, girl!" and starts laughing. Before I know it, I'm doing the same because what I love best about my Gary Daddy-o is how he always knows how to tease a chuckle out of you, even when everything's a mess. We're both shaking with laughter, until I manage to stop.

"Gary Daddy-o," I say, "Can you please get up and talk to the couple downstairs? Do we really need the cops here?"

My father sits up and swings one leg, then the other, over the bed. I look around for his jeans and see them crumpled on the floor by the bookcase. I hand them to him and he puts them on.

I take his hand and pull on it. "Come on!"

I unlock the bedroom door and Gary Daddy-o lets me lead him out into the apartment and down the stairs. Ray is walking toward the door and the couple takes a few steps toward Ray. Gary Daddy-o tips an imaginary hat while he looks at them.

"You their dad?" the man asks.

Gary Daddy-o nods.

"You live here?"

"We're staying here while his friend is out of town," I say.

The man glances over at the woman, who cocks her head at us like a spaniel.

"I was napping and the kids were locked out," Gary Daddy-o said. The man's eyes crinkle a little and I can see how he looks like his mom.

"We're visiting him from New York," Ray says, and I turn my back to the man and woman so they can't see what I'm doing. I make a cutting motion at my neck while staring at my brother. Why do we have to tell these people every last thing about our lives?

"Sounds lovely, good for you!" the woman says. "We just wanted to make sure there was no hanky-panky, climbing into the window like that."

"We're fine, but thanks for looking out for us," Gary Daddy-o says. The man reaches out and shakes his hand.

"See you around," he says, and the couple walks away as the woman leans on her son. I can see how hard it is for her to walk, but she doesn't have a cane, which I'm guessing makes things a lot harder. She's walking kind of like a penguin, and those big shoes look kind of like penguin feet. I hope her son can get her home soon, because even though the woman is on the smaller side, I bet she's not easy to carry.

At least they got my father out of bed, which is something I wish I could thank them for. I look up at him.

"Want lunch?"

"Can I go back to sleep afterwards?" he asks.

"No," I say, and Gary Daddy-o turns and walks upstairs without a word. Ray and I follow. Something makes me run right into my dad's room before he can go back inside and lock the door.

"What now?" Gary Daddy-o says.

"Nothing! I just don't want you to go to sleep again," I say.

"Too much going on right now," he tells me. "It's tiring me out."

I take a step or two closer to him, and then it hits me. I can smell alcohol on my father's breath.

"Are you drinking?"

He shrugs.

"Little wine. Nothing serious."

"We have only a little time with you. Can't you be with us this week without the wine?"

Gary Daddy-o sits on his bed, shaking his head. When he looks at me, his face is so still it's hard to even guess what he's thinking. Right now, I'm not sure whether he wants me to be here or wishes I would go. I decide to make him a tuna sandwich and ask him to come to the kitchen.

"How 'bout a little later?" he replies, but I decide to ignore that.

"Pretty please, daddy?" I say, with a big, wide smile.

That at least gets him out of the kitchen and sitting down at the table. He picks up the sandwich and nibbles at it.

"You said we could get a Christmas tree," I say. "When can we get one?"

Gary Daddy-o looks around the room. "I think there's one around here somewhere."

"Yeah?"

"A fake one."

"A... fake one." I repeat. When I was little, Ray and I would go under our *real* tree just after Gary Daddy-o would bring it home. He taught us to crouch down on our stomachs before anyone put down presents. *It's the only way you can really smell Christmas,* he'd say.

The tree always smelled like what I imagined it would be like in a forest out in the country somewhere. The smell made the air feel stronger and brighter around you. It would be the opposite smell of a fake tree and Gary Daddy-o knows that. But today, I can see how little he cares.

"They have a storage room in the basement. My friend said there's a bunch of Christmas stuff in there."

"Your friend? What's his name?"

"Nico," Gary Daddy-o says. "Gimme a sec." He walks into the living room and comes back with a key. "Go down there and see what you can find."

Ray goes down to the basement with me and we find a door with the word "Storage" printed on it in blocky yellow letters. We open the door and Ray turns on the light to see four bicycles, helmets, trunks, boxes, crates and a rocking horse that looks like it's seen a ton of better days. There's also a few kitchen appliances that nobody seems like they're using, a table with a broken leg, chairs, and a pile of tools on a workbench. Out of the corner of my eye I see something white and move closer for a better look.

It turns out to be a fake white Christmas tree that's a little shorter than my waist. There's a tiny tree next to it, but I'm hoping that isn't the one Nico mentioned.

"You think this is it?" I ask Ray.

"We could bring both," he suggests, and I roll my eyes.

"I'm not touching that one."

"Aw, c'mon, it's cute!" he says, and I kick at him and we both start laughing. Ray picks up the white tree and I help him carry it upstairs.

"Is this it?" I ask Gary Daddy-o.

He shrugs, and I decide to hope no one else owns it, even though I wouldn't want it to be my tree in a million, zillion years. *Maybe it'll look better if we decorate it,* I think, and ask Gary Daddy-o if he has any popcorn or cranberries.

"No," he says, "And I don't want that stuff anyway. I'll give you some change and you can go to the store and get tinsel."

"Where?" I ask.

All he'll say is, "Figure it out."

I can maybe ask Ruth if I'm at the bookstore tomorrow—and since she offered me a job, I will be. I hope she meant it, because that would at least give me the possibility of getting a real tree.

We spend the rest of the day trying to get Gary Daddy-o to hang out with us. He doesn't want to go to the park, but says yes to a walk "around the block," which goes on for maybe half a block before he says he's had enough. Ray tries to talk him into playing music, but no dice there, either. I make spaghetti and sauce and we toss a little cheese in, which tastes pretty good, but Gary Daddy-o doesn't eat much. I'm starting to worry about him pretty bad, but at the same time, if I admit that, I'll be *really* worried, and I don't want to get all jittery and scared.

Ray calls Nell-mom just to say hello and I try to sound my cheeriest when I'm talking to her. I tell her it's beautiful in California, and we should move there. I then tell her I got myself a little job at Inner Pages, and she gets really excited.

"I'm *so* proud of you," she says, and for the first time since we got here, I feel kind of proud of me, too. "That's really cool, Ruby," Nell-mom continues. "You're going to have to write about it in your notebook." Of course, I can't tell her about the thieves at the train station, but I'm going to try and get another one at Inner Pages tomorrow. I'm pretty sure I'll be able to do that.

Nell-mom talks a little about getting paintings ready for her show and about one painting in particular that's giving her trouble. "I'm trying to get it all one color, the face and surroundings, but still have the face stand out," she says, and I can tell she's been thinking about this for days and maybe weeks now.

While she's talking, Gary Daddy-o gets up and says he's going to lay down for a while. Before Ray and I can stop him, he's back in his room with the door locked, and my heart sinks low in my chest and even aches a little, like someone pinched it.

I give the phone to Ray and pick up a checkers set while he's talking. When he hangs up, we play a few games and watch it getting dark outside. I try to think of how to wake Gary Daddy-o up and get him to do something with us, but whenever I share an idea, Ray's eyes tell me it's not going to work. We turn on the radio and listen to jazz for a while, and then take turns in the shower, even though it's barely nine o'clock and I never go to bed before midnight if I don't have to.

I pick up the Denise Levertov book, thinking I'll get a good head start reading it tonight since there's nothing else going on. But when I'm in bed all cozy and stuff, I find myself looking at a picture on the wall with a sad-eyed, barefoot boy in the middle of a cornfield. He looks lost and about to cry and I'm right there with him. The only thing is, if you start crying it can be hard to stop, and I don't want Ray to hear me.

I turn off my reading lamp and pretend I'm at Inner Pages and there's a reading about to start. There's crowds of people everywhere, but it's still easy to pick out Ruth, and I'm imagining she's standing next to Mr. Z. *What am I going to say when I meet him?* Ruth said to ask about North Beach and what's going on around here, so I have more to write about. I'm betting I'll be too shy to ask, at least at first. But maybe that'll get easier, the longer I'm at the bookstore.

Nell-mom says you have to take your art seriously, because no one else will unless you do it first. Maybe that means having to be less shy, but what do I know? I turn over on my side and put my hands under my cheek, wondering what Ray would say. Chances are he'd say Nell-mom is right, because he always does.

I'm not tired at all right now, but I don't want to sit in the living room knowing Gary Daddy-o's hiding away in his room. I close my eyes, knowing the sooner I get to sleep, the sooner I can be at the bookstore tomorrow.

8

MAD ONES

I NEVER USE the word hubbub. It's a dumb word and I never liked it, and I'm not going to start using it now. But if you were at Inner Pages today, you'd want to use it because everyone's talking at once and there's about a zillion trillion people jawing.

Ruth says the noise isn't usual, because most people are pretty quiet in here. Only she says they're *hushed*—not quiet. It being Christmastime and all, the tourists are all excited.

I got here this morning about an hour before noon, and Ruth put me to work right away. She brought me over to a wall full of fiction books and said we needed to put everything piled on the table back onto the wall, in alphabetical order. I think that's what she was doing when I met her.

I need to put all the books back because customers come in and start reading, and let's say they look at three books and decide they only want one. They leave the books they don't want all over the store and Ruth says she finds them on chairs, windowsills, in the wrong place next to other books, on the counter, on the floor, and outside. She tries to collect them on tables they put around the store, but someone has to get them back where they're supposed to be. I've been doing this since I came in, and in the meantime, more and more and more people are waltzing around, and it seems to me that no matter how many books I put back, they're all going to get taken down again.

On the other hand, I'm getting paid fifty cents an hour plus a book of my choice at the end of my shift. I can work four to five hours a day here, my choice, and since I already learned how to run a cash register when I worked at a store in the Village, they want me to do that, too.

People are everywhere now, wall to wall. A tall chick who looks to be about seventeen is jumping up and down holding *The Subterraneans* by Jack Kerouac, which is Nell-mom's favorite book. The chick is screaming so loud her friend is plugging her ears.

Lines are so long at the register, they're having to open the door so people can keep their place in line outside. I'm in the B section, because believe it or not it took at least an hour to get through the A books. James Baldwin, Samuel Beckett, Ray Bradbury, Charlotte and Emily Bronte all have a ton of books on the table and I've got to put them back.

I've been thinking about the next book I want, and I'm going to wait until the last minute to decide, but I'm starting to think it might be Ferlinghetti's new one, *Coney Island of the Mind*. I snuck a look at it earlier and could barely put it down.

Meanwhile, everyone in here is talking to everyone else. No one is listening, but I guess it doesn't matter unless you have to hear. Which you might, if you need to work at the cash register. Luckily, right now I don't, but have a feeling that might be happening soon.

Right this minute it sounds like one of Les and Bo's parties, only louder and more disconnected. There's no music, just people pushing this way and that, getting jabbery when they find something, asking about the next poetry reading, asking if there's gift wrap and being told it's Just. Not. Cool. A man who looks about the same age as Gary Daddy-o tells a joke to a woman next to him and she about doubles over, laughing.

I'm perched on a ladder, with books in my hand and on the shelf in front of me and I've never been so happy in my life. I want to stay here forever, watching all these people choosing books and reading them, buying and discussing them. If I died and went to heaven, I think this is what it would have to be.

Ruth comes by and says they need me at the register, asking how long I can stay. I tell her I need to try and get home by around three and she says that's okay. As soon as I get to the register, it's go, go, go, and I don't even know how I'm doing any of it. Pennies, nickels, dimes, and quarters come at me in a parade of coins and I'm ringing up books and dropping them in bags every other minute.

Ka-ching! Babble. Book-look. Change.

Ring it up, put it down. Thank you.

Smile. Nod. Start again.

Babble closer, all around.

I realize I'm writing in my head and I better quit or I won't be able to concentrate. The thing about making change is its *math*, and you have to be awake to do that. Otherwise, you'll give the wrong person the wrong nickel and they'll blow their jets and everybody'll hear about it. There's thirty people on line for me and things aren't going to let up for a while.

I start getting into a rhythm, and before long I turn into a robot and it's at least an hour before I look up again. Ruth is across the room, walking a skinny guy with glasses around the store. All of a sudden someone's pounding on a counter and a man's voice says, "Hey, everybody!"

The crowd quiets down some and the man gets up on a box and starts talking. He's got dark brown hair and a white mustache and beard. He's wearing a bright red T-shirt and dark suit jacket, which is a funny combination, but it looks right on him. His gray-blue eyes are shining, and he's got a big smile on his face.

"Not so long ago, we had no idea if we'd still be open," the man is saying. "I know because I own the place."

I can hardly believe what I'm hearing, let alone who I'm looking at—but it has to be Mr. Z. He's holding up a plate of brownies and people are all quiet and listening to him, so he must be real.

"Because of people like you who believed in us, because of people like you who supported us through tough times and everything else, we're here and you're here. And it's Christmas, everybody!

The crowd around him cheers and starts applauding.

"We're putting some treats around the store to celebrate, so if you see one, take one," he says. "And thank you all for being at Inner Pages!"

Someone passes a plate of cookies over to the register and it's pretty much devoured before I can get one. I start ringing up books again and before you know it, the clock on the wall says it's three o'clock and I start thinking about how to get home. I can't see Ruth or anyone anywhere, but the guy at the register next to me says go ahead and see if I can find her, since I have to leave.

I'm feeling kind of weird about it and on the other hand, I'm bleary-eyed. Then someone standing in front of me asks if I'm a Beat girl.

"Huh?" I ask.

"Are you a Beat?"

I look up to see a boy who seems about my age, holding some books against his chest.

"Who wants to know?" I say, 'cause I like saying that.

"Just me," he replies.

"Marty, leave her alone," says a woman behind

him. As she gets closer, I decide it must be his mom. Marty is wearing a blue sweater over a collar shirt, and his eyes pretty much match the sweater. His hair is long enough so it looks Beat, but his mom doesn't seem to mind. What I mostly notice about him, though, is how energetic he seems about every little thing.

I try to see the books Marty's holding, and he catches me looking. "Coney Island of the Mind," he says.

"I can't wait to read that," I say, and he looks right at me, nodding his head up and down. "I'm trying to read all his books, in the order he wrote them," he says.

"That's cool," I tell him.

His mom watches him, without trying to make it obvious.

"Where'd you come from?" Marty asks. "I'm in this bookstore every week and I've never seen you before."

"New York," I say. "I'm visiting my dad and they gave me a job here for the Christmas rush."

"So have you been to Coney Island?" he asks.

"Yeah, I think so."

"Don't you know?"

"I think my dad took me when I was little," I say. "But I really can't be sure."

"That's okay," he says, and then turns to his mom. "Can I get a job here, too?"

"We should probably let the young lady keep working," Marty's mom tells him. She has blonde hair that she wears in a flip, and orange-colored lipstick. Her eyes are hazel-colored and she darts her face around, like she's trying to see everything at once. She also has a fur collar on her coat, so I'm guessing she and Marty are rich and do pretty much whatever they want.

"We don't want to bother you," Marty's mom says.

"It's all right," I tell her. "I'm about to get off anyway." I see Ruth coming toward me and wave, and she nods and mouths "Go!" as she moves to the register.

I dip under the counter and start walking toward the door.

"Hey, Beat Girl!" Marty calls out, which embarrasses me to pieces since now everyone's looking at us. "What's your name?"

"Ruby," I say, moving toward the door so I can get out of there before he says anything else.

"Ruby!" he repeats, "Can you hold on, just a second? I need to tell you something about your name."

"Marty—" his mom says, but Marty starts reciting a poem all of a sudden, and I can't really exit when someone's reciting a poem.

"They brought me *rubies* from the mine," Marty says, "And held them to the sun—

I said, they are drops of frozen wine— from Eden's vats that run."

"Who is that? I asked. I didn't think it was a Beat poet, but it wasn't bad.

"Ralph Waldo Emerson," Marty replied.

"Oh, yeah," I said. I'd heard of Emerson, but really hadn't read much of him.

"He used to be a famous poet. *Really* famous."

"I bet," I said, since I didn't know what to say. I like that he knows different poems and likes coming here.

I just wish he wasn't so... I don't know. I don't even know what to say about him.

"Whenever I hear someone's name, I try to remember a poem about them," Marty continues.

"How come?" I ask.

"I don't know," he says. "If I do it, I have a better chance of seeing them again."

"Oh," I say. In one way it doesn't make sense, but in another, it kind of does, if you believe in stuff like that. I mean, most people don't, but I could see someone like my friend Sophie—she's very superstitious and all that—and now, Marty.

I think of how Jack Kerouac wrote "The only people for me are the mad ones," in his book *On the Road*. In ways I can't describe but that are still very real, Marty seems a little mad. Not in a bad way, but in a way that makes him just a teeny bit more interesting. Maybe that's what Kerouac means?

"Hey, Beat girl, I hope you have fun this week in San Francisco," he says. "Maybe I'll be back and you'll be here again. When do you work?"

"I'm not really sure yet," I say. I can tell Marty's mom wants to leave, and when she looks at her son, her mouth twitches a little, like she's trying to say something but doesn't know how. She puts a hand on her son's shoulder. "Let's go upstairs," she says.

Marty doesn't look at her, and instead calls to me, "See you around, Ruby!"

I wave goodbye and squeeze through a crowd of tourists to get over to the door. Once it closes behind me, I breathe out in relief that I'm done for the day and start walking up Columbus to Broadway. It's been a while since I worked that hard for so many hours— maybe at a gallery helping Nell-mom with a show? It feels good to walk away and not have to do anything. The streets are even busier than they are back home in the Village, which is pretty wild, considering all the tourists in New York this time of year.

Getting home is becoming a breeze by now, since I know where I'm going and all. I've got my own key so I can let myself in, but when I start climbing the stairs I go a little slow because I'm not sure what I'm going to find up there. When I reach the top, the door is open and Gary Daddy-o's right there, smiling. I can hardly believe my eyes. He starts laughing so hard that I have to laugh, too.

"What," I say. "What is it?"

"You look beat, Tabeata."

"I just need something to eat," I say.

"We can do that," says Gary Daddy-o. "Ray and I were out playing today and made some pretty good bread."

"That's amazing," I say. Gary Daddy-o hasn't stopped smiling and I have no idea why, but I'm not going to worry about it. He tells me to sit down while he makes French toast, and I have a glass of juice while I'm waiting. Before I know it, he's juggling three oranges, and when I try to nab one, he stretches up his arms so I can't reach them. This is a game we played until Gary Daddy-o left town, and it's one of my favorites.

I jump up and tap one of the oranges Gary Daddy-o's holding. All of them fall onto the table, and we scramble to pick them up. "Gotta stop now," he says, smiling. I tell him about Inner Pages and realize I forgot to get a book at the end of my shift.

Gary Daddy-o peels an orange and hands it to me. "Maybe you can get two books next time you're there."

He sounds like the Gary Daddy-o I grew up with, who'd tell jokes while he was walking me to Sophie's places and stop and buy flowers for Nell-mom before he came home. If you could touch his voice, I think it would feel like velvet.

After eating, Ray pulls out a chess board from the bookshelf and asks if we know how to play. None of us do, so instead I say we should set up the board anyway and make up stories about the pieces. Ray and Gary Daddy-o love the idea, and we sit down at the table together.

I decide the White Queen wants to run off with her Knight and the Black King is trying to get back at the White King for taking his land. Ray sends the Black Knight to fight off the White one, who is trying to sneak away with the queen.

Gary Daddy-o starts playing bongos and says the pawns are getting ready to play music at the White Queen's wedding. The White Bishop gets all hepped up over this and starts jumping up and down on everyone's heads until the Black Bishop throws a pawn at him. The Black Queen says she's disgusted by everyone.

We go on like this until we get bored, and then play

a few games of charades. After that we decide to take a walk around North Beach and Chinatown and stop in a bakery where they sell thousand-year-old eggs. They look pretty old and green, even though the outside part is brown and they're in a pastry. I dare Ray to eat them, and he says only if I take a bite and Gary Daddy-o has to finish it. We agree, and when it's my turn, I think it tastes okay enough for two bites and dare Ray to take another.

Gary Daddy-o eats the rest and we all decide we need a strawberry soda, which means walking back to North Beach, but we do it slowly so we can stop in stores and ogle everything. And yeah, we all know it's touristy, but who cares?

By the time we're done with the soda, it's starting to get dark. Gary Daddy-o buys some ready-made meatballs from a butcher and we make spaghetti at home. Ray uses Nell-mom's trick to see if it's done by throwing the spaghetti at the wall. It sticks, so we know it's cooked enough.

Gary Daddy-o pours a glass of wine with dinner and then has another, but after that he stops. When he goes to the bathroom, Ray tells me that Maddie called this morning to talk with Gary Daddy-o.

"I couldn't hear what she was saying," Ray says, "but it cheered him up like magic."

"Did you talk to her?" I asked.

"Only for a minute," says Ray. "She asked how both of us were and said she misses us."

I want to know more, but Gary Daddy-o's back at the table, so I just smile and dummy up. The meatballs are delicious and remind me of how Chaz makes them at home. I think he used to have an Italian girlfriend.

I can't help thinking about Maddie while I eat. Did she and Gary Daddy-o break up, or didn't they? Some couples take vacations for a while—they call it being separated, but I think that's just for married people. Maybe Maddie wants him to come back, or maybe she wants to visit him. Whatever it is, I hope it goes the way Gary Daddy-o wants. I really liked Maddie and she was always nice to me. You never know when a parent goes out with someone how they'll be, and being a singer, you could see she and Gary Daddy-o were on the same train, so to speak.

I'd like to get him to talk about it, but I know he won't. Instead, we finish dinner and talk about what to have on Christmas. Gary Daddy-o says he made enough today to get us a roast with potatoes and green beans. We decide on buying some desserts from the local bakery instead of pie and coffee and hot chocolate. I find myself staring at the wine bottle and Gary Daddy-o sees me staring and puts it away.

"Are you going to come back to New York?" I ask, and Gary Daddy-o shrugs and says he's not sure yet.

"Washington?"

Little bigger pause this time. "Maybe."

"That'd be cool," I say, which sounds so lame I instantly regret it.

"You guys want a real tree?" Gary Daddy-o asks.

"Yeah!" Ray and I yell out, and because we say it at the same time, we need to do a pinky shake and make wishes. I wish that Gary Daddy-o will come back to the city, but I don't tell anyone. Gary Daddy-o promises we'll get a real tree and he'll be the one to find it. "Good," I say, "I wasn't sure how to make that old plastic one look right."

"There isn't any way," says Ray, and we all laugh.

Gary Daddy-o walks over to the phone and dials a number. I have a feeling he's trying to call Maddie, but no one seems to be answering and he lets it ring for a while. I watch him, hoping someone will pick up the phone, but no one does.

Gary Daddy-o drums his fingers on the coffee table and when I try to catch his eye, he looks toward the kitchen cabinets. I'm starting to feel like I wasted my wish, because I know exactly what he wants right now. No one has to tell me.

I want to keep him smiling, and the best way to do that is if Maddie wants to be with him. He knows it.

I know it.

I just hope it turns out to be true.

THE CHASE

I LOST TRACK of time for a few days, but the wall calendar in the store says Saturday, December 20. Saturday's the busiest day of the week for any business, especially before Christmas, and I was supposed to be home hours ago, but instead I had to call Ray and Gary Daddy-o to say they had extra hours for me, and that should help with a tree and all. Ray said it was fine to stay, so here I am.

Ray also told me they found a living tree and can get it if I say yes. They found it at a florist, which is open late tonight. It's planted in a big pot, and after the holiday, we can plant it in the yard. I like the idea, but I ask him how big it is. "About up to your shoulder," he says, which doesn't sound very high, but at least it's something. I think we may have enough money to get a bigger tree, but it would probably be a dead one and then we'd have to drag it somewhere whenever we're done with it.

I'm trying to decide what to do while I shelve all the books in the fiction section. I like shelving and putting new books out much better than being at the cash register. I did about three cash register hours, which nearly drove me insane. They brought in lunch for the workers, so I went to the office and gobbled a turkey sandwich and some carrots. It felt like being Santa, on a break from delivering toys.

Right now, I can hardly hear myself think over all the conversations weaving through here. There's more people squeezed into this place than I could ever imagine. I see someone at the door, which seems miles away, in a black newsboy cap—that's mostly all I can see of her, except her face. She sees me and waves, and I wave back.

Ruth comes over to help me, which makes things a little easier. "Can you stay until six?" she asks, and I say yes. She also asks if I can work tomorrow, even though it's a Sunday.

"Why would that matter?" I ask, and she smiles. I never noticed how deep the wrinkles are at the corners of her eyes, but they look really cool to me. I don't know if I can say so or if that would annoy her, so I don't say anything.

Instead, I ask if she thinks I should get a living tree or a bigger one that somebody chopped down. "We're

Jewish and don't have any trees," she says, "But if I had a choice, I'd get a living one."

"That settles it," I tell her. "Okay."

I'm shelving Bs, but getting tired and shelved a C book by mistake. Then I notice I shelved two books that start with D and pull them all down.

What's the matter?" asks Ruth.

"Nothing," I say. "Just have to start over again."

Someone at the register is being really loud, and I can hear her saying she's here to see someone. I look over there and see the chick in the newsboy cap again. She isn't in line but looks like she's headed this way. She has long, dark hair, much longer than mine, and big, dark eyes with eyelashes that are even darker.

Ruth is telling me about Hanukkah and lighting candles for eight nights during the holiday. "We make potato latkes, too. You call them pancakes," she says. I'm half listening and nod, but my eyes are glued on the chick in the cap. I'm not sure how old she is—fourteen? Fifteen? Something about her looks so familiar.

She's wearing a black leather jacket over a black turtleneck, with black jeans and boots. I'm wearing the same thing, in fact, without the jacket. I decide to concentrate on the books and see if she'll go away.

Two, three, four books go up on shelves where they're supposed to be. I climb down the ladder I'm on and pick up a few more. Out of the corner of my eye I see the chick stopping, but not to look at anything. It seems like all she wants is to stare at me.

"How do you decorate your tree?" I ask, and then

shake my head. "Sorry! What a dumbo—"

"No problem, young one," Ruth says. She started calling me 'young one' yesterday, and I don't mind.

"Is your guy Jewish, too?"

"Yep," she says. She told me she has a roommate, but didn't say much more than that. "He works in a hotel near the wharf."

"Does that mean he can stay there sometimes?"

"He's a chef in the dining room. He doesn't get free rooms or anything, but he brings home a lot of leftovers."

"Like what?"

"I don't know, shrimp, steaks, potatoes. Sometimes there's pies and desserts, but I don't like a lot of sugar."

The chick/girl/lady is edging closer. I decide to look at her straight, and see if I can make her flinch, but she doesn't seem to mind. She's a lot closer now than when she started walking toward me. A few more feet and I'll bet she starts asking me questions. People always seem to want to yak at you in a bookstore. The busier you are, the more they want to bother you.

She's holding onto something, but I can't see what it is, exactly. It doesn't look like a book, and as she gets closer, I can see it's a writing notebook. I wonder if she wants to write poetry, too. There's something really strange about it, though, because the notebook looks familiar.

"Ruby?" says Ruth. "Are you okay?"

"What?" I say. "Yeah– I'm okay."

The girl is about three feet away from me and holds up the notebook and then I see it clearly. The notebook's mine and the girl in front of me is Robber

Girl, without her friends.

"What do you want?" I say.

"What do *you* want?" she replies, and I can hardly believe what I'm looking at. Did she come here to taunt me? How did she find me, anyway? I lunge at her, trying to grab the notebook. She backs away and I nearly go flying across the floor.

"Ruby?" Ruth asks again.

"It's all right, Ruth," I say, turning to look at her. "This girl stole something—"

That makes Robber Girl turn and run toward the door.

"What?' says Ruth.

"Stole! I've got to get it back!" I yell, and everyone near me turns around to stare. I start running after Robber Girl, who's trying to make her way through all the people at the front of the store who are chatting, buying books, browsing, and trying to shush their kids while they're Christmas shopping. It's hard enough to move two inches, let alone across the floor, but this chick is doing it like she's a pro.

"Hey!" I call after her, but she's nearly disappeared into the crowd swelling around us. I can hear Ruth calling to me, but can't stop, because Robber Girl has reached the front door and is going out of it.

"No!" I call out and push through the people standing in front of me until I get to the door, too. By the time I'm outside, Robber Girl is heading to Broadway. I chase her all the way to Grant and then she hops onto Filbert, with me following. We pass long rows of houses, trees, and cars, and both of us are speeding uphill like we have wheels instead of legs.

We're going up so fast my side starts hurting and I can't believe hers doesn't hurt, too. She stops to breathe and stoops over, which gives me a chance to slow down. We're getting closer to Garfield School, which I saw when I was walking around here the day before yesterday. I get a teeny bit closer, but then she runs onto the school grounds and I have to start running again, too. I can see the windows are all dark and no one's in there, and all I can do is follow Robber Girl as she leads me further and further behind Garfield.

She ducks into an alleyway before I can catch up to her. It takes everything I have to keep running, but I do, and then all of a sudden, I'm nearly on her and she speeds up again.

She's still got my notebook, ducking this way, that way, every which way. We run further up the alley and she turns around, looking straight at me. She drops the notebook on the ground. Both of us are breathing heavily and I walk toward her, nice and slow. We're staring at each other, but no one says a word and I think, *I'll just grab the notebook and run.*

Except I can't run, not just yet. *Why is she here? What does she want and why did she drop the notebook?* Part of me wants to jump her and pound her right down onto the pavement, except I hate fighting and never want to do it again.

I got in a fight last spring at the children's home I went to and it still makes me sick to think about it. Getting all tangled up in someone else's sweat and hate is the worst thing you can do, even when you're angry—especially then. Because you're just trying to deck each other and instead of fixing things, it just makes everything worse. Fighting is about getting power over someone else by hurting them—and getting hurt yourself. It's the opposite of cool and I can't stand even thinking about it.

So.

Why am I thinking about it?

Because she and her friends stole money that Ray and I needed. Because they surrounded us when we were tired and hungry after a long trip across the country. Because all we wanted was to see our dad for Christmas and all they saw when they looked at us were easy marks. And if I didn't hate fighting as much as I do, I'd punch this Robber Girl's lights out. But I know I don't want to do that and I'm not going to do it. I just wish I knew what she wanted and why she's here. It feels so weird to be staring at each other like this. What could possibly have made her walk into the bookstore?

Of course, she would have seen the address inside my notebook. Is she trying to steal more? In that case, why would she look for me at Inner Pages? How would she even know I worked at the store unless—I don't know. Unless she was following me? This is getting creepier and creepier, and I have no idea what to do at this point.

I'm close enough to reach for the notebook and all she's doing is standing there trying to catch her breath. "You want this?" she asks.

"Yeah," I say. "I want it. I want my satchel, too.

What'd you do with it?"

"I don't have that," she says.

"Do so," I say. "You're the one who took it."

Just then, she pushes me. Not once, but twice. And then something snaps, or at least that's what they call it when you lose control of yourself. I shove her back and she grabs my shoulder. And for one split second I think, *Just tell her to leave you alone or kick her and run*, but I don't and then something in me says I have to stand up for myself. I give her a shove and she grabs my shoulder. Her face gets all dark and scary and I hit her in the mouth and then she pushes me so hard I slip and fall. It's only luck that keeps my head from hitting the ground and splitting open.

Now we're wrestling, she and me, and it's like a horrible dance you can't seem to stop doing– pinching, kicking, smacking, and grabbing each other. We roll down the alley and it's easy to tell how strong she is, much stronger than she looks. I start screaming at her, hoping that will startle her enough to let go of me.

"*Get off me– get away!*"

She doesn't answer and we keep wrestling. I've seen kids fighting outside school at home, and the funny part is now we're in a schoolyard, only no one's here because of the holiday and no teachers are going to run out to stop us. Besides that, we're in an alley and who would see us anyway? Unless a janitor's there looking out the window, but no one seems to be doing that.

I try banging my head against hers, but I think that just hurts both of us, and seems to rev her up again. I jab my elbow into her ribs and she smacks me, hard, and I scream again and try to pry her off me. This chick is good at fighting—much better than Harriet, the girl I fought with at the children's home.

Robber Girl gives me two quick slaps and before I can react, she puts her hands around my neck and squeezes. *This is bad*, I think, because once someone's hands are around your neck it's really hard to stop them if you're not strong enough.

I try to pull her hands away, but she's got me pinned with her leg and I can't move. I kick at her, but now my feet don't seem to be landing anywhere.

"Keep your mouth shut, girl," she says. "You hear me?"

I want to tell her there's no way I can say anything with her hands around my neck, but with my throat being squeezed I can't say a word. I try to look up at her but I can feel my eyes start rolling around in my head and though it seems like she's relaxing her hands a little, I still can't speak or do anything. *This is it*, I think. *If she doesn't stop choking me, I'm done for.* I close my eyes and go limp, and the light coming through my eyes goes dark.

That's when I realize– I'm going to pass out.

10

ANGEL STONE

"GIRL? ARE YOU okay? Wake up! Don't—Ruby? Please wake up! Ruby!"

I open my eyes to see Robber Girl leaning over me, her eyes wide with fear. I'm on the ground and feel pretty woozy, so I close my eyes again.

"Please wake up, I didn't mean—Ruby? Can you open your eyes again, please?"

I decide to keep my eyes closed for a few more minutes, until she goes into full-blown panic mode.

"Hey, girl, you can't die—please!"

I can tell she's getting pretty scared, so I open my eyes and look up at her. I start coughing and she helps me sit up.

"Are you okay? Ruby—"

"How do you know my name?"

"Your notebook."

"Oh, yeah." She knows my name, my address and where I work, though I can't figure out how she knew that.

"Why'd you come to Inner Pages?"

"I followed you there," she says, and I shake my head.

"I don't understand," I say. "You took my money. What do you want from me?"

"I was trying to give you back your notebook."

"*What?*"

"I read your poems and was going to your house. I saw you were leaving, but you were walking pretty fast, and I didn't catch up until I saw you go into the bookstore. I waited around outside for a while, and then I left and came back. I decided it was probably better to give you the book at the store instead of on the street somewhere."

I can't believe what I'm hearing.

"You're telling me you were trying to be nice to me?"

"I was just trying to give you back your stuff, I mean—your poetry's pretty good. I liked it."

"Then why'd you run away and start attacking me when I caught up to you?"

"You were calling me a thief and trying to get me arrested—"

"Who says anything about arrested?" I ask. "I was telling my boss you stole from me and that's why I had to leave the store—"

"You could've gotten me arrested and I could have gone to jail—"

"You *should* go to jail," I say. "You're the worst person

I ever met in my life. And where's my satchel?"

Robber Girl stands up. "The boys got that, and I can't get it back from them."

"Yeah," I say, trying to stop myself from coughing. "I bet."

"Look," the chick says. "I could have thrown all your poems in the ocean if I wanted. I tried to get them back to you because I figured you'd want them."

I watch her, trying to figure out what to say. In the meantime, she picks up the notebook and lays it down in front of me. She puts it down so gently it's like she's got something precious in her hands. And even though part of me is really mad at her, there's another part that's curious.

"What's your name?" I ask, but she doesn't respond. I try again. "You know *my* name—"

"Angel."

I laugh. I can't help it.

"Angel Stone," she adds.

"Sounds like you made that up," I say. "Like a Hollywood name."

"It's my name," she says, "And Ruby Tabeata sounds a little made up, too."

"It *is* made up," I say. "My dad's name was Tabita with an i, but he changed it because we're Beats. At least it sounds the same."

Robber Girl smiles really slightly, so I'm not exactly sure if she's smiling at all.

"My name really is Angel."

"I don't care," I say.

"Want me to help you up?"

"No," I tell her, but she acts like I said yes and extends her hand, palm up. I take it, not knowing why, and she pulls me to my feet.

"Beat Street," she says, letting go of my hand.

"What?"

Angel snaps her fingers slowly at first and then a little faster. At the same time, she closes her eyes.

"*They sprout like toadstools in the key of heat,*" she says, and I can hardly believe my ears.

"*Sweet fleet heat of the street.*"

"*Rising heat from the white of the sidewalk. And the conga sound of the Bonga bonga bongos BEAT. BEAT. BEAT.*"

By now, she has a real beat going, snapping her fingers and reciting all my words from memory. "*Every spring they sprout like toadstools in the key of heat.*"

Watching her like this, I can see there's another side to Angel most people would dig if they had the chance. I can also see it's a side she smothers.

She opens her eyes and looks at me again. "That's the one I liked. I mean, the others were good, but that's what I like best."

I want to thank her for saying that, and for returning my notebook. At the same time, I feel like she shouldn't have taken it in the first place.

"You're still mad, aren't you?" Angel says.

I don't answer, and she shakes her head.

"I lied to you just now."

"What do you mean?" I say, but I'm thinking, *I knew it.*

"I didn't start fighting you because I thought you

were going to get me arrested."

"No?"

"I mean by the time we got here I figured you just wanted to fight with me. And I wanted to fight with you, too."

I shake my head.

"What are you TALKING about?"

"You're saying you didn't want to give me a good smack—"

"That's exactly what I'm saying—"

"Come on, Ruby," Angel smiles, and this time it's easy to tell she's smiling. "You know you wanted to. And *I* wanted to see if you had the guts—"

"I hate fighting—"

"But you've done it, haven't you? I can tell, and you know what? I don't blame you. Sometimes fighting is the only way to find out what somebody's made of."

"Yeah?" I say, feeling angry again. "How'd I do?"

Angel shrugs.

"Stinky?" I ask.

"Not bad. You got some chops."

"Chops," I repeat.

"I thought so."

We stand there for a minute, not talking. I want to tell her she's out of her mind, but am pretty sure she'll just keep trying to convince me she's right. I want to tell her that even though Beats are supposed to be free and easy, it's not cool to want to pound someone. And if I did want to, I wouldn't do it unless they were pounding me first. But people like Angel want to fight everyone and they want everyone to fight them. So, what's the point in talking?

The sky seems to be getting a little darker, and I don't want to stay around here much longer. For one thing, my neck doesn't feel so hot and I'm thinking it's going to bruise up pretty soon.

"I need to go back to the store," I say.

"I get it. I just—I hope your neck's okay."

"Does it look bad?"

"It's a little red," she says, peering at me. "Maybe you should put some ice on it or something?"

"I'll be all right." I open my notebook, and even though it's weird, I look through it to be sure all the poems are still there. Angel watches me, her eyes narrowing.

"I didn't steal any."

"I didn't say you did," I tell her. "I just haven't seen them in a while, okay? I missed them."

She looks down at the ground and I close the book.

"I have to go."

"Yeah, I know."

"Where are you going now?" I ask.

"None of your beeswax," she says, and I know it isn't. But I can't help wondering what kind of place she lives in, or if she has parents or if those guys who were with her are her brothers or just some con guys she teamed up with to get money.

"Are you—" I say, and then stop.

"Am I what?" she says.

"I don't know. I was just wondering how old you are."

"Sixteen. Next week."

"When?"

"December 30."

"Oh."

"Goodbye, Ruby," she says, and I hug my notebook and nod.

"Goodbye, Angel."

She turns and walks down the alley, and I wait a minute before I follow her down the hill. I watch her going down, down, down, really slowly, getting smaller and smaller as she walks away.

"Angel!" I call, but I don't think she can hear me so I start to run. I have no idea why I'm doing this, but I can't seem to help it so I keep running and calling her name. Finally, she stops and turns around.

"What?" she asks, and I have no idea what to say to her. We stare at each other for a few seconds.

"What do you want from me?" Angel's voice is growly and low.

"Bring back my satchel and we can be friends."

"I don't need no friends," she says.

"Everybody needs them," I tell her.

Angel stands still for a second, like she's thinking. "You are one crazy little chicklet. You know that?"

"You are, too," I say.

Angel turns her back and this time I don't try and stop her. I think maybe some time, I could write about what just happened. Not a poem, but a story, maybe? I know something's going on I should write about. I just wish I knew what it was.

I turn around and start walking, not looking at anyone until I reach the store.

11

THE KICKER

"WHERE HAVE YOU been?"

Ruth isn't happy and I don't know what to say. I tried to tell her about how Angel stole all my stuff and I was trying to get it back, but she still doesn't want to say I was right.

"First of all, if she wasn't taking store property—"

"But she took *my* property. She was holding it in her hand—"

"Even so, Ruby," Ruth sighs. "You need to ask before you leave here. We're bursting at the seams—"

"I know that, Ruth. It's why I want to stay late when you ask me."

"And then walk off the job without permission—"

"It was an emergency—"

"I don't care what it was!" she yells, and heads swivel around to look at us. I can feel my face getting hot and there's nothing I can do about it.

I straighten up and look at Ruth, keeping my eyes as steady as I can. I want to talk to her just the same way I talk to Nell-mom when *she* gets mad.

"I'm sorry, Ruth. It won't happen again."

That seems to make her a little calmer, like it does with Nell-mom.

"All right. Well."

"I'm really, really sorry," I say.

"I don't know what to say at this point, Ruby, I really don't. You can't just leave in the middle of a shift at the busiest time of year."

I know enough to keep my mouth shut at this point, which is what I'm doing. She goes on for a while about Inner Pages being one of the greatest bookstores in America and how it's a privilege to be here and blah, blah, blah. Then comes the kicker:

"I want you to go home and think about what I'm saying here. If you want to keep working, come back tomorrow at noon and I'll let you know if we can still use you."

"You mean—"

"We have a lot of people banging down our doors to work here," Ruth says, and suddenly I don't like her nearly as much as I thought I did.

"So, if we still need you and you're here at the right time, we'll see if you can stay."

I nod and look down at the floor. I'm not going to

beg and plead for my job, if that's what she thinks, but I will show up tomorrow to see if she'll let me come back. I can tell there are a few people near me who are hearing every word, and I hate that.

I nod again and walk toward the door, trying not to break down in tears. A couple of older kids—I think they're maybe college students—roll in as soon as I open the door, bumping against me, but not even noticing because they're laughing so loud and joking with each other. I leap out as soon as they pass me and start walking up Columbus toward Grant. I don't feel like I want to look at Ruth again, let alone go back there. *What am I going to do?*

Church bells are chiming as I pass: one, two, three, four. I want to get home before dark, but I can't walk into that apartment and pretend nothing happened today. I walk to the park, hugging my notebook to my chest like it's the only friend I have in the world. In fact, it probably is.

The park isn't very crowded right now and I'm guessing people are mostly shopping. Plus, it feels a little cold. I sit down on a bench and open my notebook, but the words are blurring when I try to read them, so I stop.

If Ruth decides to let me go tomorrow, I can't go back in there. She's right to say that Inner Pages is one of the greatest bookstores in the country, if not the greatest. They were talking about having a reading right after Christmas, and of course I was going to go. How could I show up if I was fired?

Stupid, stupid, stupid. I just had to follow that Angel chick, who's bad luck any way you slice it. I didn't get my money back, and now I probably lost the best job I ever had, not that I had anything much before this one. I'm so mad I want to throw this notebook in the toilet, even though of course I'd die before doing that.

Someone is selling chestnuts behind me, and they smell delicious, but I don't have any money. My neck is feeling worse and I'm guessing I don't look so hot after tussling with Angel and all. I should probably go home, but it feels like someone stuck me to this bench with glue and I can't shake loose.

"Hey, girly!" I hear a man's voice and look up to see three boys coming closer to me. "What's your name?" They're all wearing black jackets and the one who called to me has an ugly smirk on his face.

That's all I need to get up and moving. I don't look back and don't talk to them, but I know it's easy enough to follow me and remember there's a church on the corner of Grant and Columbus. I start running faster, and out of the corner of my eye I think I see all three guys. I'm starting to panic a little and wonder whether I should even try the church, but there's people all around and it's the opposite of a dark alley, so I think the guys will leave me alone once I get there.

The church is big and white, like a giant monument in the middle of the street. Luckily, the door is open. I hurry inside and sit in one of the pews. There's not much light in here, but I can spy enough to see there's only two other people in the pews. Both have their heads down like they're praying.

I wait a few minutes, and then peek out the side door. There's no sign of any punks anywhere, so I slip outside and run as fast as I can to Varennes. I reach my doorstep just as Gary Daddy-o and Ray are getting home, slipping my notebook under my shirt so they don't see it. Normally I'd tell them what happened earlier, but right now, I just don't feel like it.

Meanwhile, Ray is holding a spindly potted tree, and though it doesn't look very Christmas-y, at this point I don't care and think it's got to be better than that thing-a-ma-jig we found in the basement.

"Hey, kiddo," Gary Daddy-o says, and I flash him a weak smile. I tell him and Ray that I need a shower and hurry to the bathroom as soon as I'm inside. I can see there's a couple of reddish marks around my neck when I look in the mirror, but they're pretty easy to hide with my hair. Being in the shower feels better than anything has all day, and I start to think about how to convince Ruth to keep me. Maybe if I write a letter and hand it to her?

"*Dear Ruth, I know it was wrong to leave the store today and I'll be sorry for it for the rest of my life. I don't want to make excuses, but as a writer my notebook is very important to me. When I saw this girl, who stole my notebook when I got here, holding it up and then running away from me, I had to try and catch her. I wasn't thinking about anything else and I should have been. I can only apologize and promise from the bottom of my heart I will never, ever, ever leave the store again, even if the Queen of England comes in and gives me a million bucks to do it.*

You are right that Inner Pages is the best bookstore in the country, and I'd say the world, and the writers whose books we are selling deserve to have the best clerks to sell their books and I never would have dreamed I'd be able to work here. I'm only here for another week and a half, and just being able to have had the chance to work at this store means the world to me. If you give me just one more chance, I'll work harder than anyone else in the store and work all day and all night if you need me to. I just—"

I turn the shower off and grab a towel, wrapping it around me. I said I wasn't going to beg for this job and that's exactly what I'm doing. But what else can I say to make them keep me? I feel embarrassed and ashamed and would love to tell Ruth where she can get off. But I really, truly, totally love that store.

By the time I get dressed, Ray has a chicken and potatoes in the oven and the room is starting to smell almost as good as it does when Chaz is cooking. Gary Daddy-o is putting tinsel on the tree in the living room, but the oven smells draw me into the kitchen.

"Hey," I say to Ray.

He says, "Hey," back to me.

"We're going to have to go out again day after tomorrow," Ray says.

"What do you mean, go out again?"

"Bread only lasts so long," he says, and I know just what he's talking about. "When it runs out, we have to go to the park and perform—"

"I thought we had enough for at least the week," I say.

"Not really," says, Ray, "And we want to be sure we

have enough for the holiday at least."

Of course, bread equals money equals whatever dinner we're going to be able to have on Christmas.

"Do I have to go?" I ask. "I mean what if I'm working?"

"We'll just wait until you get off," Ray replies. "People really seem to like your dancing—"

"I'm not a trained seal," I say, "and besides—"

"I know you're not a trained seal, Ruby," says Ray, his voice tightening. "But you're part of this family and we need you—"

"You're not my boss—"

"I'm your *brother*!" Ray says, glaring at me. "That's more important than your dumb boss—"

For once, I agree with him. Ruth *is* dumb, or at least she was today. But I can't let him know that, and I at least have to pretend I still have a job.

"Why are we always begging in the streets?" I say. "Why can't Gary Daddy-o get a gig somewhere? Isn't that the point of being a musician?"

"You can't get a gig every time you want one," Gary Daddy-o says from behind me. I turn around to see him in the doorway. "There's not enough gigs, and too many guys wanting them, so—"

"So," Ray says.

"We have to go out and play in the park to make money."

I don't say anything, and Gary Daddy-o keeps talking.

"Nobody knows me here yet, and that's going to take time."

"Why can't you come back to New York?" I ask, knowing it's the million-dollar question he doesn't want to answer. "You seem to have no trouble getting gigs at home."

"Ruby—" says Ray, but I hold up my hand.

"It's a good question."

"If all goes well, I may be going back to Washington," says Gary Daddy-o.

"You mean with Maddie?" I ask.

"Yeah."

"When?"

"I don't know."

I look at Ray, who won't look back at me and instead starts fussing with the chicken and potatoes. I have a feeling, though no one's said anything, that Maddie has a line in the sand going on with Gary Daddy-o, and there are conditions he has to meet before she'll let him back into her life. I'd bet anything one of them is to stop drinking, and the other may be to bring home a little more money. Though I think the first one is the main condition, and it's one he's going to have to meet.

For now, though, it looks like dancing in the park while Ray and Gary Daddy-o play sax and bongos is in my future. And even though it was kind of fun the first time, I'm not really crazy about doing it again and again and again. But as Ray says, I'm part of this family.

Whether I want to be or not.

12

BACK ROOM BLONDE

WE'RE IN THE park, and I've been dancing for about an hour. There may be another hour in me, but I tell Ray I'm going to need a break soon, and he agrees. "Let's take it easy for a few minutes," he says, and we sit down on a bench with the sax and case, which Ray closes up so no one can get to the money. Gary Daddy-o's got his bongos between his knees.

It's cloudy and dry, with a little breeze, but not too much of one, which is always good when you're playing. I'm in a pretty good mood because Ruth said they really needed me and didn't have time to train anyone else, so I got my job back yesterday. It was Sunday, but they were still open until dark, and I stayed from noon to eight doing all kinds of things, including setting up a room upstairs for a reading after Christmas.

Luckily, Ruth gave me the day off today, because she wants me to work tomorrow and Christmas Eve. I liked getting up late this morning, but at least when you work somewhere, you know you'll get paid, which doesn't always happen when you're a street performer. You have to have the energy for it, or the people watching will know you don't, Gary Daddy-o says. He has a lot of energy when he's playing, and so does Ray, but since I'm not really a dancer, I have to work at it to match them. People are tossing a lot of bills in the saxophone case, though, so we must be doing something right.

Gary Daddy-o buys us some Cokes and hot dogs from a pushcart, and we chug them down. The park has a ton of people today, and two pushcart guys get into a fight over which one is supposed to be where. I have to say, it reminds me of home. The cop who breaks them up even has a New York accent.

After that, we start playing again and things are going pretty good, when I hear someone cheering at the end of a song. I look into the crowd because someone is yelling out "Bravo," which nobody ever does for street musicians. Then, I hear someone calling out to me.

"Beat girl! Fantastic!"

I peer into the crowd, knowing Marty is the only person I've ever met who calls me "Beat girl."

"Ruby! HEY!" the voice calls out again. I walk toward the group of people watching us and then I see Marty clapping loudly and want to sink into the ground.

He's with his mom—and he looks way too happy to see me.

My face is starting to get hot and red, and I want to turn around and run home without a word. It would be just my luck this Marty guy, who I met for two minutes at Inner Pages, would be strolling around Washington Square Park in San Francisco with his mother and I'd be stuck dancing with my dad and brother, because it's the only way we can afford a good dinner on Christmas. Or really, any dinner at all.

I lift my hand weakly and wave, trying to signal to Marty that I'm not supposed to be talking to anyone. He doesn't take the hint.

"You're a really good dancer!" he says, and then Ray starts playing and Gary Daddy-o hits the bongos with his fingertips and I fold my arms, watching them. Maybe I can sit this one out until Marty goes away. *He can't stay forever, can he? Doesn't his mom have something else to do?*

I can see Ray staring at me, and Gary Daddy-o lifts one of his hands and looks at me like he really wants me to start dancing. No one is putting any money down, and people are beginning to walk away. I start dancing, moving my arms a little to look like I'm in the water, and a couple who looked like they were about to leave stay put. Marty lays a dollar bill onto the other money in the saxophone case, and his mother does the same.

We do a few more songs and then I turn my back to the people watching us and run my finger across my neck while looking at Gary Daddy-o. "Two more," he says, and we do them, only the second song lasts like twenty-minutes all by itself, and by then I'm ready to float away on a cloud somewhere, only there aren't any.

By the time we stop, though, we've got more than enough money for Christmas dinner and at least a present each, maybe two. We bow to show people we're done and most everyone claps a little and walks off, except Marty and his mom.

Of course they want to meet the family, so I introduce Gary Daddy-o and Ray. Marty actually shakes hands and I find myself wishing Gary Daddy-o had shaved this morning. I find out Marty and his mom and dad live in the neighborhood. His dad is a professor at the University of San Francisco. His mom tells us being a mother keeps her busy, and Gary Daddy-o says he knows just what she means, which is pretty funny, considering he was barely ever home when he lived with us in New York. I wonder if he can tell that neither Marty nor his mom knows someone who'd be playing music in a park or dancing in one, just to make money.

I start thinking about how quickly we can get away, but Marty and his mom are being super friendly, and Ray and Gary Daddy-o don't seem to mind. They talk about how long Gary Daddy-o's lived here and how Marty's mom lived in California all her life. She tells us her name is Vera, and takes off her sunglasses so we can see her eyes.

"We've got to run," I say, but I don't think anyone is listening.

"Got to get home and make dinner !" I say, and this time Ray pipes up.

"I can make it," he says. "If you want to talk to Marty here."

No, Ray, I don't want to talk to Marty. I don't know Marty. I never want to see Marty, or know him, or talk to him again.

"Want to show her Golden Gate Park?" Vera asks. "We could all go—"

"I really don't want us ALL to go," Marty says. "I can go on my own with Ruby."

"I don't have a lot of time—" I say.

"Well," Marty's mother begins.

"You said you wanted me to do more stuff on my own," Marty says, and Vera looks down at the ground like she's embarrassed.

"We could take a walk up to the Coit Tower," Marty adds. "I mean, that's right near here."

"I'm really supposed to be helping my brother with dinner—" I say, trying not to sound like I'm pleading.

"It's okay, Ruby. Don't worry about it," Ray says. He and Gary start walking away. Vera looks at Marty and their eyes lock.

"I'll be fine, Mom," he says. I don't like the sound of that, but I don't exactly know what to do about it, either. Is something wrong with Marty being out on his own?

Vera looks at me for a few seconds and then smiles. "Okay, Marty. If you can walk Ruby home and give me a call once you get there, I'll come get you," she says.

Marty agrees and Vera says she'll see him later.

Which is how I find myself standing next to this odd and probably rich boy in the middle of a San Francisco park two and a half days before Christmas. He's got to be rich because most poor kids don't use the word "Bravo."

Can I ditch him and run off somewhere? I could probably get away with it. But if I did, and Ray and I go back and Gary Daddy-o ever needs help with something, it seems like Vera would try to help him, if she could. So, I don't really want to make her son mad at me.

I turn to Marty. "I have time for a really short walk," I say, watching his mother leave the park along with Ray and Gary Daddy-o.

"We don't have to go to the Tower," he says.

"No—"

"Are you hungry?"

"Huh?"

"For dessert, I mean."

He seems to have found the one thing that could possibly interest me after two hours of dancing.

"Dessert?"

"There's an Italian ice place on Columbus. It's pretty close."

"Really?" I say.

"If you want to go, it's my treat."

The only place I ever had Italian ices was at Sorocco's back home, and it would be fun to have some now. I wonder if any place could ever match their ices, which taste like sherbet, only with cooler flavors, like Hazelnut. I doubt any other place's ices would be as good as Sorocco's, but like Nell-mom says when she's trying to make a decision, it never hurts to try.

"Sold," I tell him.

We start walking out of the park toward Columbus Avenue, while Marty points out different stores and cafés. He talks a mile a minute, and I'm only half-listening because I'm trying to decide if this is a date. I don't think so, though I'd love to tell Sophie I had one out here. She could never check it out one way or another, and it would make me feel better about Michael.

I didn't really think of Michael as a boyfriend. I only got to know him because Chaz has been bringing us to his family's cabin in upstate New York on certain weekends, and Michael is a neighbor up there. I loved going horseback riding with Michael and talking with him, because he seemed like an old friend, even though I only knew him a little while.

On Labor Day weekend, Sophie came with us to the cabin, and I introduced her to Michael, so we could all be friends. Sophie doesn't live too far from him now, because she and her mom are staying with her mom's producer friend Max in Connecticut.

Within a few minutes of meeting, though, I could tell Michael and Sophie really hit it off. After about half an hour, it felt like I was the odd one out. And even though I want Sophie to be happy, seeing her and Michael having such a good time together made me feel like I wasn't as important to Sophie as I used to be.

That left me feeling jealous, which nobody wants, but I couldn't help it.

The truth is, I don't want to think about it anymore. Being in San Franscisco right now with a rich boy who's taking me out for Italian ices is at least more promising than I thought it would be, even if he's a little weird sometimes.

"There's a story about this place," Marty says, which startles me because I've been tuning him out for a while.

"What's the story?" I say.

"I don't know," he replies. "I'm not sure, but maybe we can find out."

"What are you talking about?" I ask. I'm feeling a little irritated that he mentioned a story and doesn't have one.

"Let's check it out and see," Marty says, opening the door for me. No one's ever done that for me before and I can't help but like it. Then he bows and says, "After you, Beat Girl," which ruins the whole thing. I decide to ignore him and walk inside. It looks to me like we're in any old Italian ices store.

There are two or three little tables with ironwork on the chairs. A row of big, circular containers holds all the different flavors behind a glass counter. There's no one inside, but it's not exactly hot out, so I don't expect they'd be crowded right now. Besides, I'm guessing most people wouldn't be Christmas shopping for ices.

No one's behind the counter, but a few minutes later a blonde lady comes out of the back room, pulling a black curtain open briefly without saying a word and then closing it right up. She steps behind the counter and when she looks at us, it's easy to see how bored she is.

"What do you want?" she asks.

"I'll have chocolate—" Marty starts to say, and I stop him.

"You can't."

"Huh?"

If you want a real Italian ice, you need something different," I say. "Like hazelnut or amaretto—"

"We don't have either," says the blonde.

That's how I know it's not a real Italian ice place like Sorocco's.

I turn to the blonde lady. "What do you have?"

"Look at the flavors," she says. "They're written on each one."

I see lemon, blueberry, watermelon, cherry, banana, orange, vanilla and chocolate. I choose lemon and Marty gets blueberry, mostly to make me happy, I think. The blonde scoops our flavors into cups and hands them to us, with napkins. She looks to be about nineteen and is wearing tight black leggings and a long white sweater, which looks pretty cool on her. I can tell she teases her hair, which is in a high beehive style.

After Marty pays her, the blonde goes outside and starts adjusting the sign in front of the store. Marty looks at me.

"Hear that?"

"What?"

"There's something going on in the back room. Can't you hear?"

I try to get as close as I can to the black curtain at the back of the store without anyone hearing me. Marty follows, practically on tippy toes. I can hear some murmurs coming from behind the curtain, but that's all.

"Hear it?"

"Yeah," I say, "but—"

Marty lifts the curtain slightly and we peer inside. Four men are playing cards at a table. Two are smoking cigarettes and one has a cigar. It looks like a steam room in there, only there's smoke instead of steam.

"Hey!" a woman's voice screams behind us and I don't have to turn around to know it's the blonde. "Get out of there!" she yells.

The man with the cigar looks at us and leans his palms on the table to stand up. He's got a huge pot belly, and there's so much fire in his eyes I'm positive I don't want him getting any closer. Marty grabs my arm, pulling me backwards. I slip and nearly fall, but Marty catches me and we narrowly miss running into the blonde.

"Get out! And don't you dare come back!"

"Don't let him off so easy!" a man's voice booms behind us. I turn around to see the pot-bellied man, whose eyes are narrowed as his lip curls up like a dog showing you his teeth.

"Time they learned you're not supposed to go where you don't belong," he says. I duck away from him but Marty's not as quick. In less than a second, the man has his hands on Marty's shoulder. He spins him around and grabs him by his jacket collar. And by the look on the man's face, I know exactly what he's thinking.

13

SCREAMING BLOODY MURDER

I DON'T WANT to make things worse, but I know I have to do something. I run out of the store and scream, "Help!" before I remember that if you want anyone to pay attention, you need to yell, "Fire!" I point at the store and yell "Fire! Bandits!" a few times and bang on the store window. People are starting to notice and a man in a Santa suit comes closer.

"What's going on here?" he asks.

I'm opening my mouth to answer him when I hear a *boom*! I look inside and see an overturned table and the pot-bellied man kicking Marty.

"There's gangsters trying to kill us!" I say, and before I can say any more, Marty comes flying out the door. He bumps into Santa, like a rubber ball that someone threw into the street. Santa quickly grabs Marty's arms and keeps them both from falling down.

"Y'all right, son?" Santa says, while the blonde and the pot-bellied man come into the doorway.

"No problem, Santa," says the blonde, smiling. "They couldn't pay is all. I don't know what she was screaming about."

"That what happened?" the Santa man asks Marty, who is staring at the pot-bellied guy, who's staring right back.

"NO!" I scream, but Santa isn't looking at me.

Marty's nose is bleeding, and Santa asks the blonde for a napkin, which she gets and mostly throws a bunch at us. I manage to catch a few and hand them to Marty. He twists one up and puts it in his nose and I shove the other napkins in my pocket.

"Go back inside, Hank," the blonde says to the potbellied man. "We're fine."

Hank stays where he is, though, and I'm trying to keep myself from shaking when Marty turns to Santa.

"I'm okay," he says.

"You ordered without paying?" Santa asks and takes out his wallet. I can't believe this is happening, but he hands the blonde a quarter.

"Uh, you don't have to—" she says.

"I'm happy to help," Santa says. "Let's all show a little good will to each other, including you kids," he says. "You need to be able to pay for something when you order it."

"But she—he—" Marty stammers, and Santa smiles. "All right, son. I'm not going to raise a fuss, since it's Christmas time. But if you want more than a lump of coal—"

"We'll stay away from this nasty store," I say, glaring at the blonde. "And we didn't steal a thing. That guy was trying to murder us."

"She don't know what she's talking about," the blonde says, giving me the stink eye.

"Now, now," Santa says, whatever that means. Hank glares at Marty and me for a second and then turns and shuffles back into the store. The blonde follows him, locking the door behind her.

Marty looks like he wants to keep talking to Santa, but I've seen enough of these guys to know they don't want to hear about your problems. I thank this one and take Marty's hand, telling him we have to get home soon, or we'll get in trouble. That seems to get Marty moving, slowly at first, and then a little faster until we reach the corner of Green Street. I must have dropped my ice, because I don't have it, and Marty's is squished all over his shirt. Besides having a napkin jammed halfway up his nose, his lip has a little cut and I think people are starting to stare at us.

"Are you okay, Marty?" I ask.

"A lot better than I could be," he says.

"Yeah," I say. "I'm sorry."

"We've got to go back there," says Marty. "To keep more bad stuff from happening—"

"No, we don't—"

"Ruby," Marty says, "You don't understand."

"I do, Marty—"

"No, really," Marty says, and I can see he's serious. "I mean it would be all right, because I usually touch the doorknob when I leave a restaurant, and that keeps all the bad stuff that might be in there from following me."

"Huh?"

"Well, I know you don't believe it, but it's true," Marty adds. "After that guy threw me out, I couldn't touch the doorknob when we left. So now, there's nothing to stop whatever bad things might have been in that restaurant from following us home. Making things worse for us, one way or another."

"What do you mean by bad stuff?"

"Bad luck," he replies. "I mean, terrible."

"I don't know," I say. "It sounds like that 'Step on a crack and break your mom's back' stuff."

"It *is* that!" Marty replies. "But for real. I'm telling you, I need to go back to that place—"

"We *can't* go back there. We just *can't*!" I tell him.

"Then we've got to touch a doorknob on every block we pass," says Marty. "It's either one or the other."

I don't know what to say at this point, but I know it would be crazy to go back to the ices place. Touching a doorknob on every block we pass is no fun either, but it's better than going back to the store with Hank and the blonde lady. I tell Marty, sure, we can touch doorknobs on every street. That seems to make him happy, only instead of touching just one door on any given street, he's touching a bunch of them.

"Just a few extra doorknobs," he says, "to be sure we're okay."

At that point I decide to ask Marty what he knows about the ices store—mainly to amuse myself.

"What were they up to in that store, do you know?" I say. "Was it a poker game?"

"Underground," says Marty. "Underground poker."

"What's that?"

Marty touches two doorknobs that are right next to each other, since they're both part of the same bookstore. "Like regular poker, but I think it's pretty easy to cheat because no one's watching," he says. "You can make a lot of money if you're in on the game. Otherwise, you can lose your shirt and get beat up, besides."

"You think that's what's going on?" I ask.

"Don't you?" Marty says. "I mean that guy— he was really bad—"

He has to touch five more doorknobs before we cross the street, and then he starts touching all of them.

"Marty!" I yell, and he looks at me, just before touching another door.

"Why sell ices?" I ask, soft and slow.

"You know, don't you?" Marty replies, like he'd been talking normally a minute ago. "If police think it's a real business—"

"Oh. Yeah. Right," I say. "A front."

"Exactly," Marty says, and I look at his face more closely. His mouth is starting to swell up and there's a new bruise on his cheek. Luckily, it doesn't seem like he got hit in the eye, though he's starting to rub his stomach and I'm betting that's going to be pretty banged up, too.

"Listen," I say, "I've really got to get home soon. You said you only needed to touch one doorknob on each block."

"Sorry," he said. "I might be overdoing it a little."

A little? I think, but don't say it. "Let me walk you home," I say instead.

"Home," Marty repeats, squeezing his eyes shut and then opening them again. "I don't know, Beat Girl. My dad won't be home until late—he's going shopping after classes tonight."

"But your mom's there—"

"She'll be really upset if I don't look, you know."

"Normal?"

"I'll have to tell her what happened," Marty says. "We'll have to go back to that store—"

"I bet she won't make you," I say.

"She'll be upset—"

"It was an accident," I say. "I mean, where I come from, stuff like that happens all the time."

"Murder?"

"There was nobody trying to murder you, Marty," I say. "The guy caught us snooping and threw us out of the store. Period."

"Period."

"How 'bout—" I start talking, but have no idea what I'm going to say. Marty touches one more doorknob, but stops when I look at him.

"What?" he asks.

"I just—um— I was thinking."

"Thinking what?"

"Can you just touch two or three doorknobs on each block?" I say.

"Okay. Maybe," Marty answers. "I need at least three, because I didn't touch one at the ices store."

"If you can do that, we can go to my place, and you can take a shower before you have to go home."

The bruise on Marty's cheek is starting to turn purple. "Do you have a shower?" he asks.

"Of course," I tell him.

"*Thank* you, Beatie," he says. "Maybe we can think of something to tell my mom."

"You can just tell her what happened," I say. "I'll go with you and explain."

"Will you?"

"Sure," I say.

Marty looks at me. I can tell he's thinking, but I'm not sure what.

"I just want her to let me go out, Beatie," he says. "I don't want her to feel like she always has to go with me."

"I wish you wouldn't call me Beatie."

"Sorry," Marty says. "I was just trying it out."

I pull a napkin out of my pocket and try to hand it to Marty, but he stops me. "I'm okay," he says. "Where do you live?"

"Varennes Street," I say. "Only I'm all turned around—"

"I can get us there," Marty says. "We're on Edith, so I know where you are."

"Thanks."

I'm not really sure where Edith is, but I figure Marty knows where he's going, since he lives around here. He starts walking and I walk with him, and when he touches a doorknob and people stare at us, I stare right back until they turn away. As we get closer to Varennes, things start getting much quieter and I almost wonder if Marty will stop touching doorknobs. That doesn't happen, but he gets down to one or two and starts telling me about his family a little more. His mom used to be an English teacher, which makes a lot of sense, seeing what he knows about poetry. I ask him if he wants to be a teacher, too.

"What do you mean?" he asks.

"Um, I don't know," I reply. It seems like I asked the wrong question, though I'm not sure why.

"What do you want to be?" he asks.

"A writer, maybe. I mean, a poet."

"Poetry!" Marty says. "That's the best."

I look over at him and smile. "Thanks."

"You're welcome!"

"Who's your favorite poet?" Marty asks.

"I have a ton of them," I say. "Like a million."

"You really are a Beat girl, Ruby," Marty says, which makes me laugh.

"My dad used to say Beats are trying to wake people up—"

"Like alarm clocks?" Marty says, which makes me laugh a little more.

"What about you?" I ask. "Do you have any favorite poets?"

"Ralph Waldo Emerson. Robert Burns," he says.

"Any Beat poets?"

I like all the poets at Inner Pages," he says. "But I can't say who's the best."

"Okay," I say. "What about Denise Levertov?"

"I don't know her," he says.

"I'll find you something," I say. "Next time you come in."

"How long are you staying in North Beach?" Marty asks, and then answers himself. "Forever. Right?"

"Sorry, no," I say, smiling. "Just a little while longer."

"Aww," he says, and his face falls. "Now I'm sad."

"Anyway," I say quickly. "We're almost home."

We turn onto Varennes and I lead Marty to our building. He touches the doorknob before I can get my key out. Then he waits for me to unlock the door, which I do, and lead him upstairs. When we get inside, it looks so much like a scene from a Norman Rockwell painting, I do a double take.

The tree is all decked out in tinsel and ornaments. Something's in the oven, though I'm not sure what. Spots of sun whiten the walls and Ray says he's baking fish the way Nell-mom does. He starts setting the table and worse, singing a Christmas tune. "Sleigh bells ring, are ya listening?"

I turn to Marty, smiling. "Not very Beat in here today."

"Hey, Rubes," says Gary Daddy-o. "What's up?"

I can tell my dad's looking at us both up, down, and sideways. I want to head all his questions off at the pass. "We're fine," I say. "Marty wants to take a shower before he goes home. Is that okay?"

"Sure," Gary Daddy-o says. "What happened?"

"We got some ices in a store and there was a back room, and we got a little curious," I say. "We peeked in and there were guys in there playing cards. One of them pushed Marty pretty hard when he was chasing us out of there."

"Sounds kinda rough," says Gary Daddy-o, but not like it's a big deal or anything. And for the first time since we've been here, practically, I'm proud of him—being so low-key and all. Just the way a Daddy-o should be—and a real New Yorker, besides. Meaning, if you're a New York Beat you stay cool and don't get too excited about anything.

"A guy dressed as Santa came over and helped Marty up," I say. Ray and Gary Daddy-o stare at me, but I can't tell what they're thinking. "Marty thinks they were playing poker in the back."

"What?" Gary Daddy-o asks. "Where is this place? What is it called?"

"I don't think it has a name, believe it or not," Marty says. "But it's up on Union Street. They have a sandwich board outside with a sign about the ices."

"Isn't that something," Gary Daddy-o says. "I used to play cards a lot in New York. With friends, I mean."

"This didn't look so friendly," Marty says.

"Anyway," I say. "Can he take a shower *now*?"

"Of course," Gary Daddy-o says.

I show Marty the bathroom and take a towel out of the hall closet for him. Once he's in the bathroom, I go back to the living room and sit down.

"We did pretty good today," says Gary Daddy-o.

"Great," I say.

"Sorry your friend got hurt."

"He's all right."

"Were they really playing poker? Or did you just think so, maybe?"

"The curtain was open a little between the store and the back room. We could see inside—"

"You want to show me where it is sometime?"

"No," I say, narrowing my eyes. The last thing I need is my dad to go in there for a card game.

"What's the matter?"

"Nothing!" I shout. But I'm starting to wish I'd never said anything at all.

"Something's making you yell at me," says Gary Daddy-o.

"Promise you won't play poker like that."

"Why d'you think I would?"

"*Promise* me!" I yell, even though I'm trying not to.

"I won't," Gary Daddy-o says.

That's pretty much the end of the story at this point, because Gary Daddy-o has a rule about not getting too jazzed-up about stuff. If I was at Nell-mom's, everything would be a lot more dramatic, and she'd want to know every single detail of my day. Plus, you can never make her promise anything, because *she's* the grownup and *I'm* the child. But here in North Beach, Gary Daddy-o's in charge and we stay cool about things. Even when it's weird out there.

Ray gets up to finish setting the table and Gary Daddy-o watches him.

"Should we invite your friend for dinner?"

"I don't know," I say.

"Maybe he can tell us more about the city and stuff," Gary Daddy-o says. I'm about to say, "Sure," when the phone rings. Gary Daddy-o picks it up and after a few seconds, says, "Hi, babe," and I realize he's talking to Maddie.

Ray asks if I want to sing Christmas songs later and says he needs my help remembering them. We try to figure out what tunes we actually know and then which ones we like, which is a much smaller list. Ray says he likes "Santa Baby," sung by Eartha Kitt. I like that one, too, because it's funny. If I had to pick a favorite carol, I'd pick "Have Yourself a Merry Little Christmas." I like it because even though the words are sort of happy, the tune is sad, and I like when songs surprise you and do the opposite of what you think they're going to do.

"Wow!" Gary Daddy-o shouts, but I'm not sure if it's a good or a bad shout. "Six months, huh?" He walks to the corner of the room, dragging the phone cord behind him.

I know it's really dumb to eavesdrop and I don't want to, but I can't really help creeping closer to where Gary Daddy-o is standing. I can hear him fine, but all I hear on the receiver end is Maddie's voice, and it's impossible to know what she's saying. Gary Daddy-o mostly says, "I'm so proud of you," and "This is amazing." Then he says, "But it's you, so why am I surprised?"

The sound of the shower keeps going, and I can hear Marty singing to himself. *How long is he going to be in there?*

Gary Daddy-o is saying goodbye and hangs up. I scoot into the kitchen, so he doesn't think I've been standing there all this time. Ray is pulling the fish out of the oven and I pretend to be all excited and tell him what a great cook he turned out to be.

"Thanks, Ruby. Jo-Jo and I talk about starting a restaurant one day."

"No kidding!"

"We'd take turns making dinners and I could play sax while people were eating."

"In Chinatown?" I ask, because Jo-Jo lives in Chinatown.

"Or Little Italy," Ray says. "We'll see." He turns to Gary Daddy-o. "Ready for dinner?"

"You go ahead," says Gary Daddy-o. "I may take a walk for a bit."

"What did Maddie say?" I ask, because there's no point in pretending someone else called.

Gary Daddy-o gives us a half-smile, though it doesn't reach his eyes.

"She got a great opportunity, to, uh, you know. She's going to sing with Art Blakey."

Ray's face practically explodes. "THE Art Blakey?"

"You got it. New York, New Jersey, Washington, Chicago, all around for six months. I told her she has to go, and she knows it."

"That's amazing," Ray says, and I want to be happy for Maddie, I really, really do. I'm just not sure what Gary Daddy-o will do in the meantime.

"What does that mean for you going to Washington?"

I ask him.

"I don't know," he says. "We'll have to hold off on that, I guess."

Just then, I hear the water finally turn off in the bathroom. Ray tries to persuade Gary Daddy-o to eat, but he keeps saying he'll get something later. After a few minutes Marty comes out, looking cleaner than anyone who's ever been alive so far.

"I thought you were going to be in there forever," I say, and he looks at me, smiling. I'm not even sure if he can tell how mean I sound—but I just want him to go home right now.

"You have a nice shower," says Marty. "I like it in there."

"Yeah," I say. "It's just, other people need to take a shower, too—"

"Can I stay a little longer?" he asks, ignoring me.

"Sorry," I tell him. "We have to eat now and to be honest, I'm exhausted."

"I thought you said you'd explain to my mom," Marty says, and my heart sinks a little.

"I can do that," Gary Daddy-o says. "I mean—it happens sometimes. People can get angry, and that's not your fault."

"But if my mother gets upset—"

"I won't let her get upset," Daddy Gary-o says. "You and me, we'll talk about it and figure out how to make it sound like it wasn't a big deal."

"Really?" Marty asks. He takes a big breath in and then lets it out. "That would be fantastic."

"Yeah," I say, thinking Gary Daddy-o will make it

sound like nothing much, because he's good at that. And Marty's mom will believe Gary Daddy-o because he just has a way with people.

"Thank you!" Marty says. "I'm on Edith—56 Edith Street. It's not too far from here."

He slips on his jacket, and I find myself hoping that maybe having to talk to a parent will make Gary Daddy-o feel like one, too, and keep him out of bars and poker games. He'll probably keep his promise about playing poker, but I don't know that he'll stay out of any bars he comes across—or a liquor store.

Gary Daddy-o opens the closet door and grabs a raincoat that looks like it belongs to whoever owns this apartment, though it's not raining. He tells us he'll be back soon, and Ray says we'll save dinner.

I think about apologizing to Marty for my shower comment, but instead I wave my hand limply and then pull some plates down from the cabinet, knowing Ray and I will be having dinner alone.

"Merry almost Christmas!" Marty calls, and I glance at him and say, "Thanks." I turn back to the baking pan full of fish, thinking of Nell-mom cutting up peppers and onions and sprinkling them on top. She never liked to cook much, but for some reason she likes this one dish and when she makes it, everyone gets all excited and it's a really big deal at our house. I'd rather have spaghetti, but what can you do?

"Merry almost Christmas," Ray says to Marty, and I start thinking about how Judy Garland sounds when she's singing "Have Yourself a Merry Little Christmas."

"Let your heart be light," she sings, making me remember how you can see the light going out of someone's eyes—and how Gary Daddy-o's eyes went flat when he talked to Maddie, like Coca Cola when the fizz wears off.

"Bye, Ruby," Marty says, and I say "Bye," without turning to face him. I look at the fish instead, feeling really lucky that no one can see my face. I know my eyes aren't flat like Gary Daddy-o's, but they're stinging—and it won't be long before those stings fall down my cheeks.

14

ONE IN A MILLION

IF THIS STORE gets any busier, it's going to sink into the ground. But the door keeps opening and hardly anyone's going out, while more and more people are coming in. I worked eight hours yesterday, and now it's Christmas Eve, and more and more people are jamming in here like it's a prank to see how many of them can fit inside. One of the clerks keeps saying "Yo, Ho, Ho," and we keep hoping he'll go home, but of course he doesn't.

Luckily, none of us have to wear red or green—in fact everyone who works here is in black, more or less—and nobody has to be all smiley and cute. We can just be ourselves.

Another cool thing is we get a game to play for

Christmas, which really makes it a Beat Christmas to me. Mr. Z thought it up and if you want to play, you have to come back here the day after Christmas to a reading as soon as the store closes. Or, if you're working that day, you just have to stay a little bit longer.

To play, we each get a partner—mine is Ruth—and we're supposed to give each other a few words, but not a full sentence. You're supposed to take those words and use them to write a poem. It has to be poetry, not an essay or a short story, and when you come in you sign your name at the desk and it's first come, first served for when you get to read. You can invite friends and family, too. Luckily there are only about twelve people working here, so it shouldn't be too crowded. Then again, whoever they invite will be here, too.

I want to read something and at the same time, I'm terrified. A lot of people here are poets who've been writing a lot longer than I have—maybe years.

"Are you out of *Coney Island of the Mind*? I can't find it." A lady is tugging at my arm and I tell her we have them, but I've got to pull it out of our stash in back. On the way to the stockroom, a guy with white hair in a flannel shirt stops me and says he's looking for everything that was ever written by Ernest Hemingway. Great. I show him the Hemingway section and his face lights up like a fireworks display.

Gary Daddy-o didn't come home last night.

I don't know where he was, but I know he wasn't in his bed when I got up to go to the bathroom because the door was open. When it was time to leave for the store, I didn't see him, either. Before I left, I sat down on the couch trying to will Ray into waking up, but my brother's favorite time for sleeping is morning, so I had to give up. I'm hoping Gary Daddy-o will be at the apartment by the time I get there later on. I really don't want to have chase him down tonight.

I start trying to think up all the reasons why Gary Daddy-o should move back to New York, and how to convince him he needs to be around his old friends and family. Then I remember I'm supposed to find the Coney Island book and rush toward the stockroom before anyone can stop me. I have no idea how I'm going to find the lady who asked for it, but I have to try.

Right before I can duck into the stockroom, three giggly girls ask me if I ever met Jack Kerouac. I want to tell them yes, but if I do, I'll have to tell them the whole story of meeting Jack at a party and meeting him again at a reading and how I read a poem for him and blah-blah, it'll never end and that lady won't get her book. I say I never met him but hope to one day, and the girls leave me alone.

As soon as they turn away, a couple more people call out to me at once, saying, "Miss!" "Excuse me, Miss!" and "Excuse me." I turn toward the closest one, who turns out to be Marty.

"What are you doing here?" I ask.

"Not trying to bother you," he says. "I just wanted to say… say, um. The shower."

"Um. What?"

"At your house—"

I can tell he still feels bad about taking a long shower and that makes me feel bad, too.

"It's fine," I tell him. "Don't even worry about it."

"I guess I'm just in love," he says, and I can feel my eyes going wide and my eyebrows lifting.

"What?"

"I mean with the whole Beat thing," he says, and my eyebrows go down as I let out my breath.

"I always wanted to grow up in a family of artists," Marty adds. "Mine is so—you know. Plain."

I want to tell him he's anything but plain, but don't know how. He's not exactly average, but if he was in a Beat family like mine, I'm not sure they'd care very much. Nell-mom is busy with her art, and Gary Daddy-o with his music. If they notice anything that seems, you know, different, they do their best to ignore it unless they want to use it in something they're working on.

Gary Daddy-o once said that most people are trying to break out of their boring old lives and follow their dreams. Beats are supposed to show them how to do it, but who really knows what that means? I think figuring out how to live is much harder than that. It's easy to follow a rule book, but once you throw it out, you still have to figure out what you want—and how to get it.

"Miss!" Someone is calling me. "I'm trying to find *The Hunchback of Notre Dame* and you're all out of them."

"Let me check in back," I say, and then two more people walk over, and I pull Marty with me into the stock room.

"Who's that with you, Ruby?" Ruth asks. *That woman has eyes in the back of her head, I swear.*

"Volunteer—" I call out to her, because everyone who works here has at least one friend who likes to visit them, and we all call them volunteers. I tell Marty to see if he can find *The Hunchback of Notre Dame* and *The Three Musketeers*, which somebody said they were desperate for. I point him in what I hope is the right direction and then look for *Remembrance of Things Past*, which is another French book by a man named Marcel Proust from a really long time ago. Ruth says a woman requested it and I have no idea if anyone found it for her.

According to what I hear, Proust used to invite people to parties and then stay home and make up stories about what they would have said. I think he must've been a Beat, even if they didn't have any when he was alive.

Marty seems to have found his books and I look all around for the Coney Island book, but can't find it. I grab the Proust and a couple of copies of *On the Road* and I lead Marty out of the stockroom. I'm trying to find the family who wanted the French books, but I can't see much of anything because the door just swung open and a fire marshal blocks not only the doorway, but the light.

"Too many people in here!" he yells.

Mr. Z yells back, "It's Christmas!"

"Still too many people in here, and we'll have to shut you down," the fire marshal says. He's got a short-sleeved navy-blue shirt and pants on, and a white mustache. Mr. Z tries begging, arguing, talking slowly and talking fast, but the marshal won't budge. Finally, Mr. Z says we'll take some of the sales outside and tells Ruth to put together a cash box. Clerks ask the marshal to let them through and then the ones with the most muscle start carrying tables outside. Marty and I help too, because it's awfully stuffy inside.

One of the clerks tries to tie a balloon to a table, but it's full of helium and starts floating away. I think it's the only one we have, so I try chasing it into the street, climbing between two cars, which are parked bumper to bumper. I lean forward, trying to grab the balloon string. Just as I put my hand around it, something catches my foot as I move. I try wiggling my ankle, but can't.

My ankle is caught between the two bumpers of the cars I'm standing on. No one else knows it yet, but I'm stuck. I can't move.

I've got hold of the balloon, at least. But I can't bring it anywhere, or bring myself anywhere, and the crowd of people behind me doesn't seem to notice except for Marty.

"Ruby?" He asks. "Are you all right?"

"I don't—I'm not sure," I say, trying to buy some time.

"Guys!" I hear Marty say, about a half inch shy of screaming. "I think my Beat girl is stuck!"

Marty, Marty, Marty. Couldn't you give me a minute or two to get free—and not have to call me your Beat girl? The next thing I know, I'm being surrounded by tons of people, trying to get my foot out of the bumpers. Of course, everyone has to tell their sister I'm stuck, and by now they figured out I work at the store, and Ruth is holding out her hand and asking me what's happening.

A man with a beret calls out, "Take your shoe off!" and three people agree with him. I want to tell them it's not so easy to pull off one of my Keds, which are tied on, and aren't very reachable right now. Mr. Z comes out and asks me if I want help from the fire marshal. I tell him, definitely not.

"She says definitely not," someone says, and then someone else agrees with the man in the beret who thinks I should take my shoe off. I shake my head, trying to let the crowd know that neither shoe is going anywhere. Mr. Z asks if we can find the car owner, but I'm betting that could take a while.

"Okay," says another man. "Can someone help me rock the car in front a little?"

"I can!" says a woman holding a bird cage. She and Marty and two teenagers start rocking the car slowly, which makes me scream. I'm not hurt or anything, but it just seems kind of drastic and I don't want to lose my foot if I can help it.

"Hold it!" says the bird-cage woman, and the rocking stops.

"Are you okay, Ruby?" Marty asks.

I am definitely *not* okay. The fire marshal is hollering at Ruth, who's hollering right back at him, and the teenagers can't seem to resist rocking the car again.

I twist my foot slightly to the right and then twist it back again, all while clinging to the balloon. Somehow, my foot feels a little less stuck and I lift it, while holding onto someone's shoulder in the crowd.

"She's out!" a man shouts, and I lift my foot and then the fire marshal picks me up and sets me on the ground and people start cheering. Marty runs over and hugs me and I'm so embarrassed all I can do is bury my face in his neck and hope no one sees what I actually look like.

"Ruby Tabeata, you are one in a million," Marty whispers, and I see Ruth trying not to laugh as she shakes her head.

"Young lady," the fire marshal says, and I get the ten-dollar lecture about not trying to climb over cars when I'm running after balloons. By this time, most people are turning back to their shopping, and I just nod at the fire marshal until he goes away. Mr. Z asks if I'm okay, and I say, "Sure, just give me a minute and I'll start working at the table."

I look at Marty, who is now applauding and smiling. I wonder if he really does think I'm one in a million and hope he gets over it quick.

"Ruby, Ruby, Ruby," he says, and I try to think of something distracting.

"I'm fine, Marty. Let's not make a big deal over this."

"Sure," he continues. "I know you have to work. I wanted to ask you something."

"Ask what?" I say.

"I was going to invite you over on Christmas Day,

just for fun," Marty continues. "And if you want to invite me, we can each see how the other one—you know. How they celebrate."

"Huh?" The noise around us is getting pretty crazy, so I'm not sure what he's asking. Does he really want me to invite him over on Christmas, and have me visit his family, too?

"It's just an idea," Marty says.

"Well, yeah," I say. "Can I think about it?" Ray does that a lot, because it gives him more time and then if the person asking him a question forgets about it, he doesn't have to say no.

"Miss!!" Someone shouts.

"Ruby!" Now Ruth is calling, and I turn around and dash over to her. She takes the balloon from me and ties it to a chair behind the table we set up. Then she smiles at me.

"Karl and Nora here are trying to find a Christmas present for their daughter. She wants to be a poet, and I figured you were the best person to help!" Ruth says.

"Okay," I say, and Ruth introduces me to a smiling couple. The Nora lady is a little taller than Karl, but they're both tall, and he hunches over me while he talks.

"Are you the best person?" Karl asks, smiling. I look up at him and try not to blink. He has an accent, but I'm not sure where it's from. Sweden, maybe?

"Yah?" he asks again.

"You bet," I say. "This store has every kind of poem you can think of."

I want to ask where he's from, but Sophie always

says that's *rude*, so I don't say anything. Instead, I lead him and Nora inside while Marty starts walking away. Out of the corner of my eye I see him stop to watch me. He lifts up his hand and waves.

I wave back, and yell, "See you soon!" I have no idea why I said that and I hope he doesn't think I'm definitely going to his house for Christmas. But waving at him seems to make his face relax, and he turns away. Meanwhile, the noise on the street continues, sounding almost like an ocean or an earthquake might if you were in the middle of it. I could stay here all night, talking to people about the books they want and the books they've read already. It's the simplest thing in the world to talk about books, and everyone in this store was born to do it.

I steer Karl and Nora to the Denise Levertov section and show them a few other favorites. Ruth passes by and says she thought of the words I can use to write my poem, if I want them.

"Give it to me," I say, and Ruth laughs.

"Afraid of the dark."

"Of the what?"

"Dark," she says. It looks like she's waiting for me to give her some words, too, and all I can think of is how crowded we are in this bookstore.

"I've got one for you, too," I say.

Ruth says, "Good!" I think of how she dodges and dances through the store, trying to get around all the books and people, and the words bubble up before I can stop them. "Spaghetti dance."

"Well, thanks, Ruby," she says, "I like that."

I want to start working on my poetry game right away, but that can't happen—I know that. I ask her how late we're open.

"Long as it takes," she says, and I nod and smile. Whatever we're doing, this store is exactly where I want to be today. I could show people all the books I've read and all the ones I want to read, and I wouldn't even have to try to get them to buy something—they've been buying all day. I want to stay here until closing, and then bed down for the night in the rocking chair upstairs. Just for a night, maybe. Or, I don't know.

Forever.

15

FROZEN

THE KITCHEN CLOCK says 11:30 when I wake up, and Ray and I decide to make scrambled eggs and bacon to see if that brings Gary Daddy-o out of his room. He usually doesn't get up until noon, anyway, because Beats are like that. But when Ruth drove me home last night, Ray opened the door and said Gary Daddy-o had been in his room since dinner time.

The good news, I thought, *is that he's home.*

While Ray's cracking eggs this morning, I look under the tree. It seems like there are a couple presents under there, but I can't tell if they're from Gary Daddy-o or Ray. I brought two books home and wrapped them in some tissue paper I found at Inner Pages last night. My favorite is a book of cartoons by Charles Addams called *Nightcrawlers*. The family in the book are sort of Beat and sort of monsters, or as Ray would say, monster artists. The other book is *The Way of Zen* because Gary Daddy-o always liked Zen and I'm hoping he'll get back into it.

Ray calls me into the kitchen, and I get started on cooking up the bacon. After about a minute and a half, it starts to smell really good in here and I can't believe even a dead man would be able to ignore it.

Somehow, Gary Daddy-o does, though. I turn off the stove and walk barefoot to his bedroom door so I can feel the carpet under my feet. I love going barefoot on carpet.

"Gary Daddy-o?" I say. No answer.

I knock on his door gently at first, then a little louder, and then I pound.

"Ruby!" Ray yowls at me from the kitchen. "Pipe down!"

I kick the door instead. This time I hear a groan from inside. "What?" Gary Daddy-o says.

"We made you breakfast," I say. "And I got you something for Christmas!"

"Gimme a minute," Gary Daddy-o says, and I have no choice but to walk away. I set the table and Ray dishes the eggs and bacon onto each plate. We sit at the table—one, two, five minutes, but Gary Daddy-o stays in his room. I look at Ray and he holds up a finger, which is what he always does when he wants me to shut up.

We wait. And wait and wait. When the eggs are past getting cold, I start eating them. The bacon's cold, too, but I don't care at this point. Ray throws his out and gets some cereal and just then, the door to Gary Daddy-o's bedroom opens and he hurries into the bathroom. I hear what sounds like coughing sounds, and then he flushes the toilet. Another minute goes by, and the shower starts.

"Should we heat up the eggs in the oven?" I ask Ray.

"I don't know."

I pick up Gary Daddy-o's plate and walk over to the stove. The frying pan is still warm, so I start scooping the eggs and bacon into it.

"Grease it up," Ray says. "Otherwise, it'll all stick to the pan."

I scoop the eggs and bacon back onto the plate and throw some butter into the frying pan. Then I slide the food back in and start heating things up with a very small flame on the stove.

A few minutes later, Gary Daddy-o's at the table. He hasn't shaved in a while, but that's mostly how he is anyway. "Merry Christmas," he says, and Ray and I say it right back to him, like little kids in school. He pecks at his breakfast, but it's still good to see him eating. When I ask if he wants to open presents, he says, "Okay."

It turns out he got us half a dozen 45 records: Chuck Berry's "Sweet Little Sixteen," Buddy Holly's "Peggy Sue," three Elvis tunes, and "Devoted to You" by the Everly Brothers. Ray got a transistor radio that looked a little used, but who cares? He promises to share it with me and I say I'll hold him to that.

The next gift I unwrap is a new black leotard, which turns out to be from Ray. I give him a hug because it's Christmas, and hey. You oughta be able to hug your brother once a year.

Gary Daddy-o and Ray read the covers of the books I gave them, which is always a good sign. But once we all open everything, Gary Daddy-o says he's not feeling well and has to lie down again. I ask if he can stick around just a teeny bit longer, but all he says is he's under the weather. I can tell he doesn't want me to keep nagging him, because he asks when we have to go back to New York.

Opening presents just now, I imagined hugging Gary Daddy-o and him giving me a little kiss on the side of my head and calling me his Ruby-shine. I almost think about asking my dad and Ray to go out for coffee and dessert if we could find anything open. It would be so much better than playing out on the street for money.

I try to catch my brother's eye, but he doesn't seem to want to look at me. Gary Daddy-o asks again when we're leaving and Ray tells him it's the day after tomorrow.

"We have so little time left," I say, trying to smile. "Can't we do something fun today?" Gary Daddy-o nods, but he's already starting to walk into his bedroom.

"I'll be up later," he promises. *But who knows what he'll do?*

I look at Ray. "My friend Marty invited us over. Wanna come?" I know Marty didn't exactly invite Ray, but I bet if I brought him over, Marty's family wouldn't mind.

"No thanks," Ray says. "I met some guys in the

building a few days ago. They have a quartet, but their sax player is visiting family somewhere. They asked if I want to jam with them a little later."

"Great," I say, though I can't help feeling a little disappointed. "Maybe I'll just go to Marty's for a little while."

"Sounds good," Ray says, and I say, "Yeah," even though I want him to go with me so I don't show up at Marty's alone. Instead, I help my brother clean up while trying to decide what I'm going to wear. Nell-mom kept pushing me to bring the burgundy dress Maddie bought me, and even though I'm kind of mad at Maddie, I think it might be fun to wear the dress. On the other hand, it's Christmas morning and maybe a sweater and jeans would be better. I don't know.

I end up deciding on a black T shirt, jeans, and a grey and white sweater. I still can't believe it's Christmas Day here and it feels so much like spring. I step into my Keds and tell Ray I'll be back later. Except I don't really know how to get to Edith Street. Gary Daddy-o would, though, since he walked Marty home.

I knock on Gary Daddy-o's door and thank my lucky stars it's open. Gary Daddy-o's lying on his back, staring at the ceiling. When I ask about Marty's place he opens one eye and looks at me.

"Just take Filbert over to Grant," he says. "Turn and walk a ways to Edith, where you want to turn left. You can't miss it."

"Okay," I say, leaning down to give him a kiss. He rustles my hair like I'm a little kid and closes his eyes. I squeeze his hand and leave the room.

Ray gives me his jacket before I go, and then starts to clean up the dishes. "Want help?" I ask. He says no, but I help him anyway. I dry the last of our dishes and watch the water running toward the drain. I can't help but hate how quiet it is in here, and hope Ray gets out soon. I don't want to think of him sitting on the couch alone, waiting for Gary Daddy-o to wake up. "Merry Christmas, Ray," I tell him.

"Merry Christmas, Ruby."

"Just promise me you'll go out and play with those guys today."

"Oh, yeah," he says, smiling. "I promise."

I give him a hug for the second time today—mainly because I need to. Ray hugs me back tightly, the way he used to when we were kids. And for a minute, just a tiny little one, we both stay close. Then Ray pulls away.

"Have fun," he says, and then, we hear a rustling in Gary Daddy-o's room and a few coughs. Both of us listen, frozen in place. *This is how it is,* I think, *we're all frozen, waiting for Gary Daddy-o.* A minute passes and then another, and no more sounds are heard.

I kiss Ray lightly on the cheek, and go.

16

MARTY CHRISTMAS

TURNS OUT IT'S a little chillier than I thought it would be. I walk up to Filbert and then to Grant, like Gary Daddy-o said. I don't really know if I'll have the nerve to ring Marty's bell, but it feels good to be out of the house right now.

I pass a man selling hot dogs from a pushcart, and he says hello, so I wave at him. I probably shouldn't have, because now he wants to talk and calls out, "Hey, little girl!" I walk a little faster and finally get to 56 Edith. I look up at Marty's house, but I can't see much of anything, since the windows all have curtains on them.

I walk up to the door, biting my lip. I ring the bell quickly and then decide I can't go in. I turn around and start walking away, wishing I'd never come here. I'm about to turn onto Grant when I hear Marty behind me.

"Ruby!"

I stop and turn around.

"What are you doing? Didn't you ring the bell?"

I nod, feeling my face turn red. Marty runs up to me, cheeks puffing. He's wearing a dark green sweater and jeans and I'm really glad I'm not in a dress right now.

"We're going to have brunch soon," he says, "And my mother always makes too much. Want some?"

"I just ate, really—"

"Smoked salmon and cream cheese on rye," Marty says, "plus chocolate chip pancakes. That's my father's specialty."

My mouth is watering, and I find myself saying yes before I can think about it. Marty practically jumps up and down like a puppy and reaches for my hand. I'm not sure why, really, but I put my hand in his and we walk back to his door.

Marty rings the bell and his father lets us in. He's wearing the same sweater Marty has, which is a little weird, but maybe regular families do that? I think about Ray calling it *square*, and try not to smile. Marty's mom, who tells me to call her Vera, is wearing a satiny-black skirt and red sweater, which makes me change my mind about dressing up. Nobody says anything about my jeans, though, and everyone looks happy to see me. I decide to just let it ride and try to have a good time.

They have a huge tree in the living room, with piles of presents underneath it. The walls are creamy-white with paintings that look like they might be originals—

oils and watercolors, and a charcoal drawing of a man who looks like a troubadour. The staircase leading up from the living room has a thick, shiny banister, the kind children slide down on in movies. I always thought my friend Sophie was rich, but Marty's family has got to be richer. I can see Marty's parents watching me, which is embarrassing. I have to stop staring at everything like I've never seen a fancy house before.

"I hope you brought an appetite," Marty's dad says with a wink. He also tells me to call him Phil, and then says maybe I should call him Mr. Phil, and Vera tells him not to be silly.

The smoked salmon they put out is delicious and the pancakes are way better than the eggs Ray and I made. I try to eat slowly, so I'm not wolfing down the food. Marty and his family don't seem to think their meal is anything special, but then again, they always know they can *have* a meal whenever they want one. Still and all, I don't want them to know there were lots of days when Ray and I had to fend for ourselves, trying to find food when we were growing up. And even though we're doing okay since Nell-mom got married to Chaz, being with Gary Daddy-o is like going back to childhood, when some days we ate pretty good, and others—not so much.

"Ruby?" Marty's dad is asking me about my family. I explain that my father is a musician, and my mother is an artist in Greenwich Village. Marty's mom and dad smile and nod, and his dad keeps saying, "How very interesting."

After brunch, Marty's mother says it's time to open presents. The last thing I want is to watch them open present after present, so I thank them for the meal and tell them I have to go. "I hope you all have a great Christmas," I say.

"Hold on," Marty says. "Where are you going?"

"I thought I'd take a walk and then go home," I say.

Marty turns to his parents. "Do we have to open everything right now?"

"Not everything," his father says.

"Can't I take a little walk with Ruby?" Marty asks. His parents look at each other and then Marty says, "Please?"

"Just a little walk, because we really need to get a start on those presents," Marty's mother says.

"Now, Vera, presents can wait a while," says Marty's dad. His mother doesn't say anything, but her eyes narrow as she looks at Marty's dad.

"We'll be back!" Marty says, and I say, "Marty will be back. I'll probably go home after—"

"Or you won't!" Marty says, and his mom looks at the thick beige carpet on her floor.

"We won't be that long. I promise," I say, but Marty says, "Maybe," and I think I'd better stop talking because I'm probably egging him on. Marty's mom winks at me, though, like she and I have a secret handshake.

"Have fun!" says Phil, and he and Vera watch Marty lead me outside. I figure there's not a lot of places to go on Christmas, but I don't want to go home just yet.

"Too bad the stores are all closed," I say.

"I know somewhere we can go that's free," says Marty. "And I think you'll like it."

"As long as it's not the poker place," I say, and Marty laughs.

"How 'bout keeping it a surprise?" he says.

I nod and say, "Okay." I have to admit he's much more adventurous than I expect a square boy to be. Even if things get scary once in a while, he's not afraid to try them.

We walk to Grant and then toward Columbus, passing buildings that are all decked out for Christmas. "Did you get anything fun today?" Marty asks.

"A bunch of records," I tell him, and then he asks me something no one else ever has.

"Was there anything you really wanted, you didn't get?"

Well, yeah, I think, *my parents getting back together, but that'll never happen in a zillion years.* I tell him about the Sputnik necklace I want instead.

"My mom has one of those!" Marty says. "It's her favorite piece of jewelry."

"Oh yeah?" I say. I'm about to ask him if he got everything he wanted or not, but right before we get to Columbus Avenue, Marty stops in front of a black door with a brass knocker in the shape of a wolf's head. He lifts it and knocks a few times, and a tall man with a coffee-colored goatee and thinning brown hair opens the door.

"Martin!" the man says in a thick English accent. "What a surprise!"

"I hope it's okay," Marty says.

"It's always *smashing* to see you!" the man says. "I'm heading to my fiancé's house for dinner in a few hours. But we can certainly go a round or two right now."

"Ruby, this is Paul," says Marty. "My fencing teacher."

Fencing! I can't believe this cat is taking fencing lessons—and his teacher sounds like a prince in a Robin Hood story.

"Pleased to meet you, Ruby," says Paul. "Do you fence?"

"Nope."

"No worries!" Paul continues. "We'll show you what we know and see what you think."

Paul leads us to a door on the first floor, which opens into his apartment. There's an ordinary living room with a green velvet couch, and a kitchen and bedroom on either side. There's also a studio at the back, with two floor-to-ceiling windows. The room is so full of light you can see all the dust flying around. There's a rack on the wall where swords are hanging, and Marty and Paul put on helmets. Paul hands Marty a sword, only it doesn't have a point to it, and instead looks like a line with a little circle at the end. Marty tells me it's called a foil. Marty says they use them so they won't hurt each other.

Once they put on the masks, Marty and Paul start fencing. They move back and forth with their knees bent, and Paul tells me they're each trying to find an opening. At one point, Marty lunges forward at Paul, but Paul stops him with his foil, and they keep going. It looks pretty much like magic, but that's probably because they're moving so fast.

Paul calls out "Thrust" and "Parry!" every now and again, and Marty lunges forward or blocks Paul when he lunges. Eventually, Paul stops and says Marty is getting too good and wearing him out. Then Marty asks if I can try, and Paul asks if I'd like that. I say yes in a heartbeat.

Paul shows me how to hold the foil and Marty helps me put on a helmet. I learn how to bend my knees and put my right knee forward over my toes. I move back and forth a little and it feels like being a dancer, only more powerful because you've got this thing in your hand. The most fun happens when Paul pulls some broadswords off the rack and shows Marty and me how to practice using them. We smack the broadswords at each other like two knights in a story about King Arthur. I think about what it would have been like if Angel and I had been using these when we were fighting. I'm guessing I would've won.

After a few minutes, Paul asks if we want some water and we both say yes, because fencing tires you out. Then Paul offers us some Coke, which is even better. He and Marty tell me about a British fencer named Bill Hoskyns who won a bunch of medals, and Gillian Sheen. "She proved that women could be as good as anyone," Paul says. I try to imagine Nell-mom looking around the city to find me fencing lessons and have to laugh. I bet Marty just had to ask once and his parents jumped at the chance to tell him yes.

Paul takes out a plate of cookies and says he baked them mostly for his fiancé, but kept a few for himself and we should taste them before we go. I'm biting into a chocolate butter cookie when the doorbell rings and the knocker sounds right afterwards. Paul straightens right up and walks down the hall to the front door.

Once he opens it, I can hear Marty's mom and dad. I try to swallow my cookie as fast as possible, because of Marty. He's trying to smile at me, but I can tell it isn't working. That kind of smile tells me only one thing. Marty's in trouble.

17

VERA SPILLS THE BEANS

A MINUTE OR two later, Paul comes back into the apartment. "Did you tell your parents you were stopping by?" he asks Marty, who shakes his head to say no. "Always a good idea," says Paul, but doesn't say more. Marty mumbles an apology, and we grab our jackets. Paul walks us out and everybody's all smiles.

"Hey, son," says Marty's father. "We thought you were just taking a short walk and coming right back."

Marty and I scooch into the back seat of his parents' Buick. Neither one of his parents is wearing a coat or jacket, which makes me think they must have left their house in a hurry. Marty's mom Vera doesn't say anything, though I can hear her breathing in and out, like she's in a windstorm. They ask for my address and Marty tells them, and in a few minutes we're at my door. I wish everyone Merry Christmas and get out of the car, but then Vera jumps out with me.

"I'll meet you at home, dear," she says to her husband. "I feel like a walk myself." Marty looks at me for a second and then looks away. "Bye, Ruby," he says. "Merry Christmas."

Marty's dad speeds off and I'm left standing on the sidewalk with Vera. Her hair is teased around her head in a bubble cut, so still it doesn't move in any direction. I look at her, wondering if I'm supposed to ask if she wants to come in, but she starts talking before I can say anything. Not talking so much as talking on the way to yelling.

"You're going back to New York soon, right?" she begins. I nod and that seems to be all she needs to keep at me, like a runaway train.

"I don't want my son seeing you again," Vera says. "Make sure you stay away from us."

"You—what?"

"You promised me you wouldn't be long. Did you not?"

"Well, yeah," I said. "But then Marty's dad—"

Vera goes on, barely listening to me. "Never mind about his dad! You saw it was time for presents—"

"I didn't—I don't—I'm sorry."

"You made it sound like you'd take a quick walk and then Marty would come right back. *That's* what we expected," Vera continues. "I know you may not have known he wanted to see his fencing teacher, but you could have at least reminded him we were waiting at home."

I can see the woman wants to put all of this on me, and there's not much I'm going to be able to do about it.

"Marty isn't like you," Vera says, and looks at me as if I'm supposed to know what she's talking about. Yeah, he's different and all, but I don't think his mom should be talking about him like this. She doesn't seem to agree, though—in fact she seems like she's been waiting a long time to spill the beans.

"He doesn't think like most of us. He'll think, all right, but it's not the way *we* do by a long shot! He wants to do things *his* way—or no way at all. Marty doesn't understand how others may feel or worry about him. And he has no idea how dangerous it can be if you—if you're wandering around and meet the wrong people," Vera says.

And I'm definitely the wrong people, I think, *because Beats want to do things our way, too.*

"We want him to have friends, because he doesn't have many," Vera continues. I'm guessing that's true about Marty, which may be why he was so excited about meeting me. But Vera keeps talking like she's reading my mind.

"We don't need him to follow some mixed-up Beatnik girl around—"

"Marty's not following me. And I'm not a mixed-up Beatnik—"

"Whatever you are," says Vera. "You broke your promise! Marty's father and I are extremely disappointed." Ugh. I guess she *had* to bring up the whole disappointment thing—guaranteed to make you feel worse than you ever imagined.

I can tell she knows she hurt my feelings and doesn't care. Or maybe she's even happy about it. Whatever she is, Marty's mom is done talking and ready to close the book on me. She turns and walks away, stomping her boots on the ground in a harsh little rhythm as she moves down the block. She doesn't turn back at all, though part of me wishes she would so I could blow a raspberry at her.

And bad as this little conversation was for me, I can't help feeling even worse for Marty. I don't know what's wrong with him or if it has a name, but his mom is sure treating him like a baby. I feel awful for him because once a parent gets a thought, it's like a dog with a bone and there's no giving up on it. And at the same time, there's nothing I can do to make things better.

I pull my key out of my pocket and let myself in. I have no idea what time it is, but when I get inside the apartment Ray is cleaning his saxophone. Gary Daddy-o is nowhere to be found, but the door to his bedroom is shut tight so I'm guessing he's still in there.

"D'you have fun? Where'd you go?" asks Ray.

"I don't know. Marty and I went to his fencing teacher's place, and that was great. But his parents got mad at us and drove me home, and his mom says she doesn't want me to see Marty anymore."

"That's too bad," says Ray, though he doesn't sound too jazzed about it.

"His mother says he doesn't think like we do."

"Weird," Ray says, but he's soaking the saxophone reed and doesn't seem like he's listening much.

"She acted like something is wrong with Marty, but she wouldn't tell me what it was, exactly. You know?"

Ray looks up from the reed and meets my eyes. "I have no clue, Rubes. I've known him for all of two seconds."

"Yeah," I say. Fair enough. But it's not like Marty wanted to rob a bank or something. I don't know. Maybe his mom is just one of those overprotective types, which Nell-mom thinks are the worst kind of parents. Probably because if Nell-mom even notices where I've been at the end of the day, it would really shock me. I don't remember her ever asking.

On the other hand, what would she say if she could see Ray and me and Gary Daddy-o right now? I don't think he even knows where his thumb is, let alone what his kids are doing. But I don't want to tell Nell-mom, because even though she doesn't know where I am most of the time, she's way too fussy about when I see my father.

I look at Ray, who's turned away from me. He's about done cleaning his saxophone, and the kitchen clock says it's close to three. That would be dinner time in New York, and I'm guessing Nell-mom and Chaz are chattering away with all their friends around the dining room table. Chaz probably made a turkey, and knowing him, it's got all the fixings and there's three kinds of pie.

Thinking about this and what happened today

makes me furious, but there's no one I can talk to about it. I decide the only thing that will make me feel better is pick a fight with Ray. This isn't always easy, because Ray's so laid back, but if I keep at it I can usually drive him crazy.

I'm pretty good at that.

Ray is putting the saxophone back in the case.

"Should we call Nell-mom and Chaz?" I say.

Ray scratches his ear. "You mean to say Merry Christmas?"

"I wish Nell and Gary Daddy-o were still living together."

Ray's mouth twitches, slightly. "Yeah, well—"

"If Nell-mom hadn't gotten mad at Mrs. Levitt—"

"That's ancient history—"

"It was April, Ray. Just eight months ago."

"What I'm saying is, no one can change it—"

"But if she had stayed cool, none of this would have happened and Gary Daddy-o would be okay."

"Why do you always blame her for everything?" Ray's voice rises, just a little bit.

"Because it's true—"

"You make him the angel when she was just trying to take care of you. She's not the enemy—"

"I didn't say she was the enemy. But if she stayed with Gary Daddy-o, we wouldn't be watching him fall apart."

"He's not falling apart—"

"He locked the door to his bedroom so he can drink all day while his kids are visiting for Christmas. If that's not falling apart, Ray, what is? You wanna tell me?"

Now my voice rises too, and it doesn't feel like I'm pretending. I mean, yeah, I may have started out wanting to get under my brother's skin, but I'm getting under my own now, too.

"What do you want from me?" Ray is yelling. "Nell-mom is human."

"I *know* that!" I yell back.

"I don't—I don't want to fight about this, Ruby," Ray says, and I can tell he's trying hard to lower his voice.

"The point is, Gary Daddy-o is alone. He doesn't have anyone who cares about him and Nell-mom's getting everything she ever wanted—"

"She wanted to be with *him*! She loved him. But you were stuck in a children's home and she had to get you out."

"Are you saying she still loves him?" I ask.

"How would I know? She's with Chaz and Gary's here, and there's nothing we can do about it. We're going home day after tomorrow."

"I'm not going," I say, and Ray looks at me, widening his eyes. The truth is, I have no idea why I said that, but now that I did, I want to stick to my guns.

"I can't leave him like this and neither should you."

"Ruby—"

"I don't care!" I shout. "He's a mess! This is horrible!"

Ray doesn't say anything, and then we hear a crash behind us. Gary Daddy-o either fell off the bed or threw something at his bedroom door, which opens. He stands in the doorway, staring at us, with the room dark behind him.

"*What's the matter with you?*" he yells. "*It's Christmas!*"

I stare at him, not knowing what to say. At least he knows what day it is, even though he's not celebrating.

"Sorry," I say, because I don't know what else to do.

"Why can't you both get along for once?" he asks. I can barely believe he's asking this question, but maybe, I think, I should answer him.

"We came all the way out here to see you."

"And I'm happy about that—" he says.

"You have a funny way of showing it," I say, crossing my arms over my chest.

"Sometimes moms and dads are tired, Ruby. I know you want to do a lot while you're here, but when you're older, you need a little rest now and then."

Yeah, but it's not resting when you're holed up in your room for days, I think. I want to tell him he's scaring me because now and then when I catch his eye, it looks like nothing's in it—like my Gary Daddy-o went away and left a dead man in his place.

I want to ask him if he remembers all the fun stuff we did in New York when he was home, like telling fortunes with Nell-mom's tarot cards or going to a party at Les and Bo's, or inviting friends over for dinner. We'd all stay up half the night, playing records and dancing.

I want to ask him if he'll ever take me shopping in Little Italy and chat up all the storekeepers like he used to, or race me home to the corner of Perry and Bleecker Streets. But I can't because I'm afraid of what the answer would be—even if he pretends to say yes to it all.

"What do you want me to do?" Gary Daddy-o asks, and suddenly I know exactly what to say.

"I'm supposed to read a poem at Inner Pages tomorrow. Will you come?"

"Sure, we'll come," says Gary Daddy-o. "Won't we, Ray?"

Ray won't look at me and I know he's still mad. But he nods, very slowly, which is something.

"What are you going to write about?" Gary Daddy-o says.

"I don't know yet," I say, which is true.

"Okay," Gary Daddy-o replies. "I'm going to lie down for a little more."

"Don't you want to have dinner with us?"

"Later," he says, and closes the door to his bedroom. I hear the sound of the lock latching, which means he probably won't come out until morning, or maybe he'll wait until noon.

Ray and I look at each other. "I'm going out for a walk," he says. "I'll be home before dinner."

"Right," I say, and Ray slips on his jacket and hurries downstairs. I watch him from the window, half hoping he'll turn around and wave. I've got to start working on the poem, so maybe it's lucky that I have some quiet time. Maybe that's what I've been missing—time to write.

The only problem is, I can't seem to get myself to do it. All I want to do is lay down in bed like Gary Daddy-o, and close the curtains, so it's dark.

18

THE VISITOR

I WAKE UP early, thinking about how I meant to call Nell-mom and forgot. I was up really late writing and have no idea if any of it was any good, but at least I tried. The last thing I want is for anyone at the bookstore to think I'm an idiot, but at the same time, if I walk in there without a poem, I'll be an idiot for sure.

Nell-mom says that anything you do can be improved if you sleep on it and take another look in the morning, and I've already done the sleeping part. Before I take a look, though, I'm going to call her and make it sound like I'm having the perfect holiday.

I dial our number and Chaz answers. I tell him Merry Christmas and we yak for a while. He tells me about the dinner he made, and his friend's new baby, born on December 25. By the time he puts Nell-mom on the phone, Ray is starting to wake up and make coffee.

"Hey precious," Nell-mom says, which always makes me cringe, but there's only so much you can do with parents.

"Hey, Nell-mom. Did you have a good Christmas?"

"Good as it can be without you here," she says, and I feel sad, because it doesn't feel like Gary Daddy-o would even think to say something like that. At least right now.

Nell-mom is asking me what we did, and I think about making up stuff about a special dinner and Gary Daddy-o playing music, and us singing jazzy-type Christmas songs. But when I look at Ray, I feel like he wouldn't have it in him to lie, and Nell-mom and Chaz already think I make up too many stories.

Instead, I say I saw a new friend and we had some family time, and I'm working on a poem to read at Inner Pages today. Nell-mom is all excited about that and makes me promise to read it to her as soon as I get home. I say, "Sure!" and then hand off the phone to Ray.

Once he and Nell-mom start talking, it's like they're old friends, chittering away in what I've come to think of as their own secret language. Ray is telling Nell-mom about Telegraph Hill and all the winding streets around here, and the coffee shops and Beats everywhere. I can't hear what she's saying, but when Ray says something about a North Beat Christmas, I can hear Nell-mom laughing loudly.

Of course he got that from Gary Daddy-o, but Nell-mom thinks it's something Ray made up by himself.

I'm feeling a little jealous because even though Ray and Nell-mom have their own way of talking, I used to have something like that with Gary Daddy-o, too. But who knows where it is now—or if I'll ever find it again.

I go back into my room, grab a pen and hop onto my bed, propping the poem up on a book. I don't like anything I've written, so I crumple up the paper and throw it onto the floor. Just even thinking about writing right now feels like I'm in the middle of a jungle, with huge leaves smacking me, no matter where I try to move. I hear Ray saying goodbye to Nell-mom and hanging up the phone.

I think about the words Ruth gave me to write about—afraid of the dark. That was one of the things Gary Daddy-o taught me when I was younger. I always wanted to turn the lights on at night, and he'd say no, because it cost too much money. "Nothing wrong with the dark," he'd say. "It's just daytime, going to sleep."

We're supposed to go home tomorrow, but what happens if we do? I think of Gary Daddy-o in his room, alone, or lying on the floor of the living room like he did when we first got here. Does he even know how much I love him? I don't know.

Then something makes me get up and look through the pockets of the jeans I was wearing on the train with Les and Bo. Somehow, after all this time, the piece of paper Bo gave me with his number on it was still there. I pull out the number and luckily, I can still read it.

Now, I just have to call Bo without anyone else knowing. I'd like to tell Ray, but I know he'd be embarrassed about asking Bo for help. I understand, but at the same time I don't think Bo would have given us his number if he didn't want to be there when we called.

Gary Daddy-o's in his room, but Ray's pulling leftovers out of the refrigerator and starting to make some eats. I think the phone cord is pretty long, so I start carrying the phone as slowly as I can to my room. It barely reaches, but if I dial it outside the door and pull the receiver inside, I think I can talk to Bo without Ray knowing.

I'm getting close to my room when Ray calls out to me. "Whatcha doing?"

"Calling Marty," I say, and that seems to satisfy him because I don't hear any more. I crouch down next to my door, dialing the phone number Bo wrote down for me. After a minute, I can hear the sound the phone makes when it's ringing, and then a lady answers.

"Hello?" she says.

"Hello!" I say, opening the door to my room and stepping quickly inside. I close the door as much as I can, trying not to squish the phone cord, and when I talk it's in a low tone of voice so no one in the apartment will know what I'm saying.

"I can't hear you. WHAT?" the lady asks. She sounds kind of crackly and it seems like it's just as hard for me to hear her as it is for her to hear me.

"Is Bo there?" I say, trying to raise my voice a little.

"Honey, you need to speak louder. Did you say you're looking for Bo?"

"YES," I say, giving up and yelling because what else can I do?

"Just a moment, miss. Let me call him to the phone," the lady says, and I let out my breath while she looks for him. Except she comes back to the phone and asks who's calling.

"Ruby," I say.

"Who?"

"Ruby!" I scream, and the lady, who I'm guessing is Bo's grandmother, comes right back at me with a yell of her own.

"All righty! Hold on!" She puts the phone down and calls out for Bo.

After a minute or two, I hear his voice on the line. "Hello?"

"Bo, it's Ruby," I say.

"Course it is!" he says. "Merry Christmas!"

"Merry Christmas, yeah. I hope your grandmother isn't mad at me."

Bo laughs. "She's mad at everybody when they interrupt our time together. Don't you worry about it. You havin' fun?"

"Yeah," I say. I tell him about working at Inner Pages and his voice warms up. "No kidding! I'm so proud of you!"

We talk a little more and then I decide it's now or never if I'm going to ask for help. I ask Bo if he meant what he said about calling if I needed him, and he says, "You bet, honey. What's up?"

I tell him as much as I can without saying that I think Gary Daddy-o is falling apart. I think he figures it out anyway, because he asks if I want him to come out and help. I tell him I don't want to mess up his time with his grandmother, but I'm not sure what to do with Gary Daddy-o.

"Don't you worry about it," Bo says. "Your daddy is family and he's feeling bad right now. He needs help and he needs his friends."

Hearing Bo talk makes me want to cry, but I don't want anyone here to see that, so I clear my throat and keep talking.

"When could you come?"

"I can leave tomorrow," says Bo. "Les will want to come, too."

"Your grandma will hate me—"

"Don't you worry about it, Ruby. I told you. We should be able to be there by the twenty ninth, but you can go home earlier—"

"I don't want to leave him and besides, I have to let you in—"

"Your mama's going to be expecting you. And she'll be mad at me if you don't show up at home."

"I could leave my key with a friend at the store, maybe."

"That's a good idea! You do that," Bo says. Just talking to him like this makes me feel normal in ways I haven't for a while.

Bo asks for Gary Daddy-o's address and I tell him how to get a bus from the train station in Oakland. "I don't think Ray wants me to call you," I say.

"Just go home with Ray and you don't have to say anything," Bo says. But I still feel bad about leaving Gary Daddy-o.

"Okay," I say. "Let me think about it. And Bo?"

"Yeah?"

"Thank you."

"You bet, honey. Any time."

We hang up and I bring the phone back into the hall. I wish I could ask Marty to hang out here all day and let Bo in, but his mom won't let us talk any more. I could ask Ruth, but then I have to tell her what's going on with me and my dad. Or I could just stay here and let Nell-mom be mad about it.

I sit down on my bed, looking out the window. I hate it when I have to make decisions, because how are you supposed to know when you're making the right one? Sometimes there are no right decisions, and you have to choose one anyway. I *hate* that.

I stand up and open the window, leaning on the sill to look at everyone on the street. No one was around yesterday, and there's only a little girl pulling on her dad's hand as they come out of the building across the street. He's holding a blue teddy bear and she has a candy-cane colored bow in her hair.

I watch the dad and his daughter until they get to the corner, when someone in a kerchief passes them. It's a lady holding a little box wrapped in silver paper with a red bow. I can see little blonde hairs flipping up under the kerchief and as she gets closer, I can see she's wearing sunglasses.

She keeps walking and it looks like she's headed toward our building. I lean over the windowsill a little more, and then she looks up at me and waves. She points to the box she's holding, and I can't believe what I'm looking at.

She's smiling and it looks like she wants me to come downstairs and let her in, which I'm never in forever going to do.

She stands outside the door waiting; I let her wait. She waves at me again and I watch her without moving.

"Ruby?" she calls. I step back into the bedroom, moving backwards until I'm sure she can't see me. I can still see her, though, crossing her arms over her chest. She must think I'm coming downstairs to open the door, but I'm not and never will.

Not for all the tea in China, as Sophie's mom would say.

Not for that—

Or Marty's mom.

19

SPUTNIK

AT THIS POINT, Vera finally figures out I'm not going to let her in and rings the bell, and of course Ray bounds down the stairs and opens the door. I can hear them chit-chatting away like they're old friends as they walk upstairs together, and I know it'll be just a minute before she walks in here. At least Gary Daddy-o's asleep and she won't see him. But she won't see me either, because I'm not setting foot outside my room.

Ray calls out, "Ruby?"

I don't answer, so he calls again.

"What, Ray?"

"Marty's mom is here."

"I know."

"Wanna come out?" Ray asks.

"Nope."

"What?"

"I'm not coming out, Ray."

"Wha—"

"It's all right," Marty's mom says. "I just want to leave this for her."

"Ruby," Ray says again. "What's the matter with you?"

"It's really all right," Ray's mother says. "I just want to leave this and I'll be on my way."

Before she leaves, I decide to make Ray eat his words and throw open my door.

"What are you leaving?"

Marty's mom turns around. She puts the present on the coffee table and turns around to look at me.

"You don't have to open it if you don't want," she says. "But I was very unfair to you and I'd like to make up for it. If you want to throw it out, you can. I mean, I hope you'll enjoy it and visit with us one last time before you go."

"I doubt it," I say.

"Well," she replies. "I didn't mean to blame you for being Marty's friend, and that's all you were doing. I'm—I tend to be overprotective sometimes, and I shouldn't be. In any case, I hope you enjoy the gift if you decide to unwrap it."

Marty's mom turns and walks to the door, which Ray opens for her. She waves and goes downstairs, and I stare at the present while Ray follows Marty's mom downstairs and lets her out.

Gary Daddy-o, meanwhile, hears none of this,

which is fine by me. I sit down on the couch and stare at the present, trying to see if I can force myself to throw it out the window. Except I just don't get enough presents to make me want to do that.

Ray comes back inside the apartment and closes the door. "Looks like she was sorry for whatever she said—"

"That doesn't make it better," I say.

"Everybody says stuff they don't mean," Ray says. "Especially you."

"She was so ugly with me," I say. "I can't just decide I'm going to like her after the stuff she said."

"She's apologizing. She brought you a present."

"That's to make her feel better. Not me," I say.

"Nobody's ever given me a present like that."

I shake my head and sit on the couch, folding my arms so I don't pick up the present. Ray plunks down next to me.

"Gonna open it?"

"I don't know."

"Come on, Rubes."

"I told you I don't know," I say.

"Can I open it?"

"No."

Ray reaches for the present. "Why not?"

"*Hey*—"

"Come on, let's see what's in there!" He grabs hold of the present before I can stop him.

"Let go—"

"Someone's gotta open it—"

"That someone is me!" I yell, reaching for the

present while he stands up and holds it over my head.

"Are you saying you want it now?" he asks, and I stand up and reach for it.

"Yes!"

"You sure?"

"Give it to me!" I'm practically screaming, and surprised Gary Daddy-o hasn't woken up. Ray hands me the box and I pull it away from him and turn, practically running into my bedroom.

"Where you going?" he calls.

"It's mine!" I yell. "I get to open it without you."

I slam the door and push the little button in the doorknob to lock it. Once I sit on the bed, I slide the ribbon off the box and unwrap the present slowly. It may be junk, but I have a feeling it's going to be a really nice present and I want to open it carefully, so it feels like a real surprise. When the last of the wrapping paper comes off, there's a small velvet box with a hinge. I open it and gasp, because I can't believe what I'm seeing.

Marty's mom gave me a necklace. Her Sputnik necklace.

It's way more beautiful than mine was, with Sputnik balls all along the front speckled with rhinestones. I can't believe she wanted to give me such a fancy piece of jewelry like this. Does she think that makes up for what she said?

Probably what she really wants is for me to be friends with Marty again. That may be the only thing we agree on, because it seems like she over-protects Marty all the time, which can't be all that good for making friends. I can tell he's lonely and *needs* to pal around with someone his own age. I have no idea what Vera said to Marty about me, but I at least wanted to say goodbye and all that before I leave. It looks like I can do that now, since Vera apologized.

If I do go to Marty's house to tell him I'm leaving, I'll have to accept Vera's apology, I guess. I can try to give her necklace back, though, since I don't exactly like her. I could also ask Marty to hold on to my key. All I have to tell him is Les and Bo are old friends and coming out to see my dad for New Year's, and I want them to be able to get into the apartment in case Gary Daddy-o's out running errands when they arrive.

Yeah. That's what I'll say, and I need to say it soon. I open the clasp of the necklace and put it on, looking at myself in the mirror. It's the coolest necklace I've ever seen, and I might as well wear it over to Marty's if I'm going to give it up soon. I look at myself again, thinking a necklace like this needs earrings to go with it. Luckily, I brought my hoopy ones, and put them on.

"You ever coming out of there?" Ray says, and I tell him to hold his horses. I put on some black jeans and a leotard and comb my hair, which was getting pretty ratty. By the time I come out, Ray is eating a turkey sandwich in the kitchen.

"Wow!" he says. "Marty's mom gave you that?"

"Yeah," I say, trying to sound like I could care less. "So what?"

"So *what?*" he laughs. "You should at least thank the lady for the necklace."

"I *know* that," I say. "But I'm going over there for Marty, not her. And I may give the necklace back—"

"You're not going to do that," Ray says.

"It's none of your business, Ray."

Ray puts his hands up to show me he doesn't want to argue. He warns me not to stay out too late, because we've got to pack tonight to be ready for tomorrow.

It's starting to rain a little and I have to look down while I'm walking. I'm starting to know my way to Marty's house, so I don't even have to look at the street signs. By the time I finally get there and knock on the door and Vera lets me in, Marty is practically jumping up and down and cheering, which makes me wonder what Vera may have said to him.

Vera invites me to have lunch and says she wishes Marty's dad were at home, but he had to go to work. We sit down at the table and Vera looks at me and smiles. I smile back, because I'm not really sure what else to do. "Your necklace looks beautiful on you," she says.

"Thank you," I say. "But I really want to give it back to you—I don't have a place to wear it—"

"Oh, please take it, Ruby, please? I never wear it anymore—"

"Yeah, take it, Ruby! My mom and I want you to have it," Marty says.

"Marty—" I begin, but he gets louder and closer. "You've got to take that necklace, Ruby, I know you're going back to New York and if you don't take it, for sure I'll never see you again."

I have a feeling this is like that doorknob stuff we

went through after we left the gambling place. Marty must be really superstitious, and if I don't take the necklace, it's going to upset him a lot, which I can tell by the expression on his face.

"You can't leave it here, Ruby. Marty would never let me wear it—"

"Okay, okay," I say, and I have to admit I love the necklace and don't mind keeping it. Marty and Vera look relieved, and we start eating the cream cheese and salmon bagels, which are beyond delicious. But as we're talking, I realize I can't tell Marty about Bo and my Gary Daddy-o. and give him the key without Vera finding out somehow—she'll just ask him about it, if she has to, and he'll tell her it's for my dad's friends. She'll start asking questions, and if Bo or Les stop by, she'll ask them, too, and who knows where that'll end?

I just don't want this family to stay involved in my life. I don't want Ruth or anyone at Inner Pages involved, either. I have to find someone, though, before I leave tomorrow. The only other idea I have is Marty's fencing teacher, Paul. I have a feeling if I asked him to hold the key for Les and Bo, he'd just do it, no questions asked. English people are pretty careful about stuff like that, aren't they? At least in books and movies.

I sit up a little straighter, watching Marty's mom cutting up slices of a chocolate cake. I think Paul is exactly the right person to hold onto this key right now—and his house should be easy to find. I'm pretty sure it was on Grant—the only house on the street with a black door and wolf's head knocker.

We talk a little more and then Marty asks if I'll write to him when I get back to New York. I say yes, as long as he writes back. He wants to know if the bookstore is open.

"Definitely," I say, "I'll be stopping by there tonight to get my pay and they're doing a reading when they close. Just the employees and maybe their families or something."

"Oh, Ruby," Vera says. "Will you be reading?"

"I think so," I say. "But it's really no big deal."

"It is to *us*!" Vera says. "Can we pretend to be family and come to the reading?"

"I don't know," I say, feeling my face get red as I think about how many people are going to be at this reading.

"We'd love to be there, wouldn't we, Marty?" Vera says, and Marty nods his head and says, "We'd love to!" at the top of his lungs, which makes me laugh so hard I have to sit down.

"Why not?" I hear myself say. "We close at nine tonight, so you'll want to come in before then, because they're locking the doors when the reading starts."

"We'll be there with bells on!" Vera says. I can't help thinking of what she said about being my "pretend family" and wondering what it would be like if that were true. Yeah, they'd be square, but they'd also show up if you were doing something special.

Ray is mostly with his girlfriend Jo-Jo when we're at home. Nell-mom is way wrapped up in her painting, and Chaz cares a whole lot about her and just a little about us. And right now Gary Daddy-o is a mess—so I don't know if any of them would come to a reading if I was in it.

Marty's mom asks if I want another slice of cake and I imagine her baking the cake while Marty and his dad play checkers in their den. I think Nell-mom would rather die than make a cake, and I'd probably die if I tried to eat it.

I tell Marty's mom I'll have to pass on the cake this time and she promises to meet up with me later. We say our goodbyes and I walk down Grant Street toward Columbus, looking for the fencing teacher's door. I still haven't finished my poem and I'm not sure I can before the reading. But with Marty and his mom coming, I feel like I really have to try.

I can see the black door and my heart starts pounding while I try to think of what to say to Marty's fencing teacher when I see him. I grab hold of the wolf's head knocker and rap it once, twice, three times against the door.

No answer. I rap again, and then see the fencing teacher's face at the window. He comes to the door and opens it, looking down at me with a slight smile.

"Hello there! Isn't this a surprise!" he says, and his English accent seems even cooler than it was when I met him yesterday.

I look up at him, wondering how tall he must be because he's taller than Gary Daddy-o and definitely taller than Ray.

"Looking for Marty?" he asks.

"I'm… no. I'm not," I say. "I'm looking for you."

"Yes?" he waits expectantly, and I try to think of how to ask him about the key, as casually as I can. He might ask why I don't want to share the key with Marty, and how would I answer?

"I suppose you want to talk about fencing," he says, and as I meet his eyes, I decide a little fencing talk will buy me some time before I tell him what's really going on.

"Um, can you recommend any teachers in New York?"

"I'm sure I can, if you give me a moment," the man says. "Would you care to come in?"

"Uh, sure," I say, and he opens the door and tells me to step inside. I watch him go downstairs and lean against the wall, looking at an umbrella stand in the corner. I'll get his recommendations and then leave, I think, because I can't give this man a key to our apartment.

I can't give it to anyone, and I can't have Bo and Les coming into that place by themselves with my dad, like he is, in the bedroom. I need to be there, and I need to open the door when my father's buddies knock on it.

Because whatever kind of family I wish I had, I still have a real family and Gary Daddy-o is the heart of it. I need to be there for him. And I will.

20

POETRY NIGHT

INNER PAGES CLOSED about an hour ago, but if you asked me what time it was, I'd have no idea. Five people read their poems already, and I'm up after the guy reading now. Nobody famous is here yet, which is a good thing, because if someone like Allen Ginsberg walks in while I'm reading, I'm going to run right out.

Mr. Z stopped me today to say thank you for pitching in over the Christmas rush. How many bookstore owners would say that? I came in at about three and have been here ever since. Ray's here with Marty and his mom and dad, but Gary Daddy-o's nowhere to be seen. Ray said he tried to wake him but had no luck.

Normally I'd be hurt, but the poem is kind of

about what's going on with my dad, so maybe it's all right he's not here to listen to it. I pretty much wrote it on the fly, which is why I'm so nervous. Normally, it takes weeks to write a poem; I keep going over and over them like Nell-mom does with her drawings, so by the time she starts painting something it's like she's drawn it a hundred times.

I was just so turned around by everything that happened since I got to North Beach, I couldn't think, let alone sit down and write something. The next thing I know, Mr. Z is starting to introduce me to the audience, and I'm hoping no one sees my hands shaking by the time I get up to read.

"This young lady stopped by our store about a week or so ago, visiting from New York," Mr. Z is saying. "We were desperate for help, and she very kindly agreed to work with us. So I want you to give a warm welcome to Ruby Tabeata—what's your phrase, Ruby?"

My voice sounds jangly and jerky, even to me. "Dark."

"What?

"I mean," I manage to say, "Afraid of the dark."

"Fascinating!" says Mr. Z. "Let's hear it."

Now I'm even more nervous because my poem is anything but fascinating. I walk slowly to the front of the room and the guy who just read his poem lowers the mike for me. I step forward and pull out a piece of paper, glad that all I have to do is read from it and don't have to look at anyone who's watching me. The last time I said a poem out loud was who knows when?

Maybe when I went into that stupid House Committee meeting to try and help Sophie's mom, when she was accused of being a Communist.

What I really want to do right this minute is run to the door—but then I see Marty. He's been restless, which I mostly expected because he doesn't like being in the same place for long. He was outside with his dad for a while, but when Marty saw me through the window, he wanted to come in again, so his dad opened the door and in they went. I decide to look right at Marty, because that way I can pretend it's just us in the room and I'm reading my poem to him.

Marty is looking straight at me, waiting. I look down at my poem and read.

"Let's go around the block, you said

Don't be afraid of the dark

And I said I wouldn't be but

I always got tired because we'd walk and walk and walk from here to everywhere

I loved holding your hand

We'd always stop somewhere, and you'd sit down jamming with your friends

You said Don't be afraid of the music

Sweet, sweet sound of pain underneath our lives

I said I wouldn't be afraid since

I knew that was what you wanted to hear

But I could hear that pain like the sound of the ocean on Coney Island

*Whatever you do it'll come for you, but we don't talk
  about that*

Don't

Don't talk

*And by the time we got home everything was dark and
  you said*

Shhh

Don't be afraid little girl

And I was only three and said I'd

No, no, no

I wouldn't be

Then five, then six, then eight, then ten

Then now when I'm really afraid but not of the dark, just

Afraid

Of you not being there when I need you

I need you all the time

Afraid of needing you. Like I do.

Marty's still as a ghost and quieter than he's ever been. I lower the paper and stop reading, and people start to applaud. Everybody's applauding after every reader, and it's not a contest type thing so I have no idea what people are really thinking. I start walking back to my seat, and Ruth stands up and says she hopes everyone made copies of their poems because the store wants all of us to leave their writing (if they care to), before the readings end. Since all the writers I ever knew said to make copies of your work, I copied the poem twice—once on the paper I'm using now and once in my notebook.

I start walking back to my seat when Ruth calls to me. "Aren't you going to leave your poem with us, Ruby?" My face turns red as a beet as people in the audience start to chuckle. I put the paper down on a table at the front of the room where everyone else's papers are, and then scoot back to my seat.

The next person reading is one of the guys who was mostly at the register, and he's reading something about stock car races. I'm so relieved to be done that I can finally start breathing, and when Marty's mom walks over, she hugs me like we've been friends forever. I can't tell what Ray's thinking because he won't look at me, but I have a feeling he's mad. We listen to about ten more people and then everybody gets up and starts milling around, having coffee or soda and desserts, and a few people break out wine bottles, and Marty's mom takes a cup and drinks one. Marty wants to talk about my poem and keeps asking what it means. I tell him it was just an exercise and doesn't mean anything.

I don't know if he gets that or not, but when he asks who I'm writing about, Ray wheels around and stares at me. "Just a guy I know," is all I say, and Ray turns away as soon as I say it. Marty doesn't press me, so I ask him if he wants to split a Coke. He says yes and I lead him to the refreshment table, where I pick up a bottle and pour it into two cups. Marty breaks off some brownies and puts them on a plate.

Marty's mom has been talking to Ruth for a while and by the time she comes back she's all gushy about my poem. "'That was really something, Ruby,'" she says. I smile weakly and thank her, and then say I've got to go to the bathroom because the one thing I hate doing more than anything in the world is talking about writing, especially mine.

Everybody knows you shouldn't talk too much about writing anyway—it's bad luck. And when people ask what you're working on, you can tell they have this fairy tale idea of what it's like to be a writer—or any kind of artist. They don't want to hear that you have to put whatever you're feeling and thinking about into words and find a rhythm and something to drive your ideas through that rhythm like a go cart. They just want to hear that you wake up in the morning and this stuff pops into your head.

It looks like not only Marty's mom, but other people are coming up to me, too, and I've got to get away from them. I zip over to the bathroom as fast as I can and when I come out, I find the guy who was reading after me telling a joke and join up with everyone listening. When they laugh, I pretend to laugh with them, and I can see Marty and Ray and Marty's mom and dad across the room, talking to Mr. Z. I'm glad they're over there and I'm here, and I get a little more Coke and keep laughing, while the guy who read after me keeps talking. He's telling a story about a customer who couldn't find the book he wanted and made this guy go all over the store—only he's making everyone laugh while he's talking. I wish I could do that.

A little later, Marty and his parents come over and

say they've got to take off. They ask about bringing Ray and me home and I say yes. Ray's nowhere to be found, though, so I spend at least ten minutes searching the store to see if I can find him. Finally, Marty tells me he's standing outside, looking in the window at all of us. I don't even ask why, because I've never been able to figure my brother out.

Marty asks him, though, and Ray says he just wanted to see what we all looked like from the outside in. I roll my eyes at Marty, who has to try really hard not to burst out laughing.

Meanwhile, Ray follows Marty's parents to their car, which is parked at the end of the block, and in a few minutes they're in front of the store and Marty and I hop in the back seat. It doesn't take long to get us home, and when we get there, I look up at the window and everything looks dark—so I'm pretty sure Gary Daddy-o must still be in his room.

I thank everybody for coming to the reading and taking us home, and then Marty and I promise to write each other. I can see Vera smiling behind Marty's head, and thank both of them for making my Christmas better.

"Will you come back?" Marty asks. "Next Christmas, maybe?"

"I don't know, Marty—"

"You have to. Please?" Marty says, and looks at me with such big puppy dog eyes I say I'll try.

"Don't forget me, Ruby—"

"How could I forget you?" I say. All I can really

think about is Gary Daddy-o and trying to get out of the car as fast as possible, but I know I've got to say something that will satisfy Marty. "I'll try as hard as I can to come back, Marty, I promise."

"You can stay with us, if you ever need to," says Vera.

"Well—thank you!" I say, and Vera holds out her hand. I shake it, and then jump out of the car. Ray steps out onto the curb and thanks Marty's dad and mom for driving us home. Marty's dad says you're welcome, and finally drives away. Marty waves and I wave back, and Ray starts turning his key in the lock when I stop him.

"Hold on, Ray."

"What?'

"I need to tell you something."

"*What?*" His voice rises with impatience, and it almost seems like he knows what I'm going to say.

"I, um. Yeah."

"Ruby—"

"I can't go home with you tomorrow."

"You have to."

"No I don't, Ray. You can't make me."

Ray is furious, I know, but if we're going to have a fight, I'd rather do it out on the street than inside, where Gary Daddy-o can hear us.

"We promised Nell, for one thing—"

"Les and Bo are going to be here in a couple days and I need to let them in," I say.

"Are you kidding?" Ray asks.

"They told me to call if I needed them—"

"We don't need them—"

"Yes, we do, Ray. We can't do anything without them."

"What exactly do you think they can do?" Ray folds his arms, which I can only see because of the streetlight overhead. I can see his eyes squinching up, too.

"They can help him get better," I say.

"How, Ruby?"

"I don't know, Ray! I just know we can't do it, and Bo and Les are his friends."

Ray kicks the door, but I don't say anything. He kicks it again.

"What do you want to do, stay in North Beach?"

"No," I reply.

"Then wha—"

"I'll leave the day after they get here," I tell him.

"Les and Bo."

I nod, and Ray kicks the door again. I tell him to stop it and he does it another time for good measure.

"You know I'm not going to leave you here alone."

I swallow before answering. "I'm not saying you have to stay—"

"I *have* to," he says.

I shake my head. "You can do whatever you want."

Ray shakes his head, too. "We've got to call Nell," he says.

"I know, but we can't tell her why we're staying—"

"Yes we can—"

"Please, Ray?" I look up at him with my most pleading face, hoping he can see it in the dark. "She'll never let us near him again if we tell her what's happening."

"You don't know that—"

"I know our mom—"

"You don't know ANYTHING about her!" Ray yells, and someone across the street opens his window and shouts at us to shut up. I roll my eyes and Ray keeps talking.

"Whatever she did by marrying Chaz was for us," Ray says. "*She* was the one who got you out of the children's home and she's been the one taking care of both of us ever since we've been born. She loved Gary Daddy-o and so do I, but he's on the road all the time and *she* was the dad *and* our mom. You blame her for everything, and it's never been fair."

"Okay, Ray, so it isn't," I say. "But Gary Daddy-o is still our dad and we can't let him fall apart like this."

Ray doesn't say anything, and he's so quiet I can hardly stand it. I put my hand on his arm and he looks down at me. Only his eyes aren't sad, they're hard. I mean, hard and dark like marbles, only they'd be made of ice.

"I used to be like you," he says. "I wanted him to stop drinking, and I kept thinking he would. You have no idea how many times I'd meet him somewhere for a gig and the band would be waiting and he wouldn't show. And then Maddie gave him the world on a string and what did he do with it? Start drinking again. And she said it broke her heart."

"He just wasn't over Nell-mom," I say. "He can find someone better—"

"He's not going to find anyone until he stops drinking," says Ray. "And who knows if he's ever going to do that."

"Ray—"

"And now you've got Les and Bo coming for nothing—"

"Bo said he could help, and that's all I need to know," I say. "And, hey, you should go back to New York tomorrow if you want—but I'm telling you. I'm waiting until the twenty ninth."

"You're really something, Ruby."

"I don't care."

"*You're* going to call Nell-mom, you hear me? Whether you make something up or tell the truth—you're going to talk to her."

"I will—"

"And if she asks me—"

"You better not rat me out," I say.

"You think I'd rat you?" Ray says, and his eyes look even harder than they did a minute ago. "I don't have to rat you!"

"I didn't mean—"

"You'll just write a poem about it and tell the whole world anyway!"

I stand there, watching Ray's lips move as he twists his mouth. *Did he really say that?* Of course he did, and I can't even answer, because I don't know what to say.

Ray turns away. He unlocks the door and trudges up the dimly lit stairs. I have no choice but to follow him up and inside the apartment. He walks straight into his room, slamming the door. In normal times, Gary Daddy-o would wake up and ask what's happening, but we all know these aren't normal times.

I sit on the couch, staring at a picture of fruit on the

wall. It's orange, but I think it's some kind of tropical fruit, with a name I never heard of before. I close my eyes and lean back. I can't help but think about what Ray said just now, and it's giving me goosebumps, even though I don't call him on it.

"*I used to be like you.*"

Does that mean he doesn't care anymore about his own father?

And then accusing me of sharing all our business with the world, which I never do, which I couldn't.

I write about what I'm living through, and if you didn't know me, you wouldn't know who I'm writing about. Ray was being nasty, and he hurt me. But he wasn't being fair.

And yeah, nothing about life is fair, but why did he say that? Why do people say the meanest things they can when they're angry?

Now it's my turn to stomp to my room and close the door. I don't really care what Ray's thinking right now, if he's even thinking anything.

Because, you know what? I'm tired of all this. I'm way too tired to figure it out.

21

PLAYLAND

TURNS OUT NELL-MOM is kind of quiet when I call the next morning. "What are you doing?" I ask her.

"Just being," she says, and then doesn't say any more.

I decide to try again. "Are you okay?"

Nell-mom clears her throat. "I don't know if I'll keep painting."

"Huh?"

"It's a lot of time and I get very little notice for it," she says.

"You always tell me *not* to give up," I say, but Nell-mom doesn't listen to her kids, so she stops me right away.

"We don't have to talk about it, Ruby. In fact, I'd rather not."

Yeah, I think. *What else is new?*

"Well, anyway," I say, "I just want to tell you we'll be a few days later than we said."

"What?" she says, and I can hear a little panic in her voice.

"I had to work most of the time I was here, and we hardly did any sight-seeing," I say. I hate myself for lying, and at the same time I know if I told her what was happening, she might get upset at my dad for a really long time. I know lying is a habit, and it's hard to break the more you do it. At the same time, I don't know how to make adults be reasonable about things like who their kids can love and stuff. The only way out of it is to keep lying.

"What do you want to see?" asks Nell-mom.

I tell her about Fisherman's Wharf and the Embarcadero, redwoods in Golden Gate Park, Russian Hill, and then Chinatown.

"We really want to celebrate New Year's Eve with you," she says.

"Can't we celebrate right after?" I ask. "New Year's Day is Wednesday, and we should be there. We can pretend it's New Year's Eve and go out to a restaurant on Thursday, maybe? School doesn't start until the week after, I mean, we can do anything we want."

"Yeah, well. Maybe," she says, and I can tell I'm not thrilling her.

"Beats don't have to be like everyone else, right? That's what you and Gary Daddy-o taught me and Ray."

Nell-mom sighs. "I guess I taught you pretty well."

"Yeah."

"Promise me one thing, okay? You won't get on that train any later than December 30."

"I promise," I say, and she answers very quickly. "All right." She sounds a little down, and I think about what Ray said about her holding everything together. Is that why she wants to quit painting?

"Can I talk to Ray?" Nell-mom asks.

I lift the phone and point it at my brother, but he signals me that he's not talking. I tell Nell-mom he's taking a walk and hang up.

Ray is making bacon and eggs, and it smells so delicious I want some desperately, but am afraid to ask. I try looking at the wall pictures again, then stick my head out the window. After a few seconds, I come back inside and do a handstand, but all I can think about is bacon until I'm practically foaming at the mouth.

Ray turns off the burner and pulls some plates down out of the cupboard. "I can tell you want some," he says. "Go on."

"Are you kidding?" I ask.

"Why would I be kidding?" he replies.

"I thought you were mad at me."

"Well, you can be really annoying," Ray says. "But it's always a waste of time to be mad, specially at Christmas. So."

"So?"

"You can have some bacon and eggs."

"Thanks, big brother."

"Yeah—"

"Thank you."

I roll up my pajama sleeves and dig in, and just then the door to Gary Daddy-o's room opens and he moves toward us like a bear coming out of hibernation. He's got three five-o'clock shadows, it seems, one on top of the other, and his eyes are bleary and red, but he must be smelling the bacon and eggs, too, because he's definitely shuffling toward us.

"Hey, you," he says.

"Hey, Dad," Ray answers. I want to tell Ray what Nell-mom said about painting, but don't want to get into a whole discussion about it. Maybe he knows already, anyway.

I wave and smile at Gary Daddy-o instead, and Ray asks if he wants some breakfast. That's when I get an idea.

"We want a little more time here so we can look around a little. Maybe you can show us your favorite places."

"I don't have a lot," he says.

"At least one," I say, thinking if he shows us even one thing, that'll mean I was telling the truth to Nell-mom.

Gary Daddy-o rubs his eyebrow and looks at me. "I know we didn't get to see much—with you working and all."

"It was just too busy," I say, "and we hardly had any time with you."

Gary Daddy-o looks down at his hands. He speaks so softly I can barely hear him. "Sorry."

"Please, Gary Daddy-o? Let us stay just another day or two and go somewhere? I mean who knows how long it'll be 'til we're together again. Right?"

Still looking at his hands, Gary Daddy-o's voice is a teeny bit louder. "Lemme think—"

"Somewhere fun—" I tell him.

"What about Ocean Beach?" he asks. "It's beautiful—"

"Yeah—"

"And you know what? Right next door is Playland—"

"Playland!"

"And you know how much I love amusement parks."

It's true. Ever since I was little, Gary Daddy-o borrowed a friend's car and brought us to New Jersey every summer for a trip to Palisades Park, which happens to be the best amusement park in the world. It has food stands where they sell ice cream and cotton candy, kiddie rides, a fun house, roller coaster, pool, and all sorts of grown-up rides that make you scream.

"I don't have a lot of money—"

"I've got some," I tell him. "I can spend all of it because they still owe me for this week. I was going to stop by there later."

"Yeah?"

"Come on. Playland!" I yell, making Gary Daddy-o laugh. He stands up and says he'll just have to take a shower. He goes into his room and comes out a few minutes later, like he said he would. His shower is quick, and even though I smell a teeny bit of whiskey on his breath, he smiles like the old Daddy-o and even gets Ray to smile when he fake-boxes at him while I'm doing dishes.

I decide it's a Beat day and put on jeans and a black

top, with a long black sweater. We take a few buses to get there, but San Francisco is smaller than New York and it's quicker to get around here. Nobody's talking much, so I yak to the bus driver, who is friendly enough to ask where we're from and where we're going. "Have fun with Laffing Sal," he says, but won't say more than that.

Laffing Sal turns out to be this enormous statue at the entryway to Playland. She's in a glass box and has red hair and freckles and a space between her two front teeth. I looked up at her, wondering what's so special about her—and right at that moment she bursts out laughing like someone's tickling her, only super-loud because she's as big as a house. She's laughing so hard I can't help laughing back at her. Ray and Gary Daddy-o laugh, too.

With a little bit of my money and a little of my dad's, there's enough for a game or two and a treat. We walk around the midway a while and have ice-cream sandwiches and cotton candy. Ray tries the shooting gallery, and then Gary Daddy-o and I try, too, but don't win anything.

I want to go in the Fun House, which has all kinds of mirrors that make you look spooky, and a turntable that throws you off if you don't hang on to it. Gary Daddy-o used to love funhouses, but today he's having none of it. I try talking him into it, but then I see the carousel and it's a whole lot easier to get him to ride on that than it is to do anything else.

We get on the carousel every year at Palisades Park, and it's always been one of my favorite rides. When I got to be four or five, Gary Daddy-o always put me on the bigger horses and rode right next to me, while Ray and Nell-mom rode behind us. Nell-mom mostly picked a white horse, and Ray picked a blue one. Mine was always black if I could help it and Gary Daddy-o didn't care about the color he had.

Today we find a black horse for me, a blue one for Ray and brown for Gary Daddy-o. Once the music starts, I feel like I'm a little kid again, just listening to the tunes they play while we go round and round. All around us are what I'd call fairy lights, and I just can't help smiling from ear to ear. Gary Daddy-o and Ray are smiling, too.

When the music stops, I ask if we can go again, but Gary Daddy-o says we don't have the money. I ask if we can run around for a while and he says sure, but first he thinks he needs a bathroom. I do, too.

We find two right across from each other and I walk into mine. A bunch of different ladies are in there and all of them are staring at me. I guess it's because I'm all in black and in pants and they're all in skirts or dresses. There's a long line of ladies, so it takes me a while to get to a stall. By the time I come out, there's just a few people in there, including a mom showing her daughter how to wash her hands. I wash mine and use a paper towel in a basket to dry them.

The sun is so bright when I come out of the bathroom, I have to shield my eyes. Ray is standing there waiting for me, but I don't see Gary Daddy-o.

"What's he doing?" I ask.

"He's on that bench over there," Ray says. "He says he's not feeling well and has to go home."

I can't help feeling disappointed, especially as I wanted to go to the beach. I walk over to Gary Daddy-o and sit beside him.

"What's wrong?" I say.

"I don't know," he says. "Just not feeling well."

"Can I get you some water?" I ask.

"Nah—"

"Just a little water to see if you feel better?"

Ray squints at the sun as he looks at us. The corner of his mouth twitches a little and I can tell he thinks I'm barking up the wrong tree, but I keep trying.

Meanwhile, there are swarms of people everywhere. Families with moms and dads holding their kids' hands and lining up at the carousel and roller coaster. I imagine holding Gary Daddy-o's hand when I was younger, standing on line with him for a ride.

A little boy holding a stick of half-eaten cotton candy says his stomach hurts and his mom says he ate too much. The boy starts crying and his mom throws the cotton candy out and tells him next time, she won't buy him any. A lovey-dovey couple are walking toward the bench in front of the little boy, with their arms around each other. They veer off to the shooting gallery and we watch the man try his luck so he can win a prize for his girlfriend. Another couple pushes an older man in a wheelchair and that makes me turn to Gary Daddy-o.

I ask him if he'll try sitting for a few minutes, and Ray gets water from one of the food booths. I go back into the bathroom to wet some paper towels and try putting them on his forehead, but he waves me away. I ask if I can find him some ginger snaps, which always make him feel better at home. But he says no, and pretty soon we're walking out of the gate while Laffing Sal screeches behind us.

There's nothing sadder than an amusement park. Is there?

Out of the corner of my eye, I see a man walking around with his family, looking at his watch. He has a pink shirt on, which you never see, but that makes me decide he's nice, and I ask him what time it is. He says it's half past two, which means there's enough day left for the beach. You can see and smell the ocean from here, and it reminds me of how much I love the ocean, which always smells like freedom to me. I promise myself that I'll ask Nell-mom and Chaz to take me to Far Rockaway when I get back. The cool thing is, I know they'll do it, and I won't have to keep asking them. But right now we have to take care of Gary Daddy-o.

As we board the bus, I can see Gary Daddy-o is sweating. He's also starting to shiver a little and his face seems paler than it was a few minutes ago. Maybe he has a fever or something? Ray's looking at him, too, and asks if he's okay. Gary Daddy-o says he's fine, but has to lay down for a while as soon as we get home. Then I hear the worst sound I ever heard—even weirder than the sound Laffing Sal makes. It's Gary Daddy-o's teeth chattering, like he's freezing. I can't even describe how bad it sounds.

Luckily, we only have to walk a few blocks to Varennes Street after we get off the bus. By the time we start walking, Gary Daddy-o seems like he's about to keel over, and Ray and I have to walk beside him. All of us hook arms and walk slowly, so Gary Daddy-o doesn't fall.

"What's the matter?" I ask. "Should we get a doctor?"

"No need," he says. "I just have to lay down."

He's sweating like crazy now, and his face seems hot when I touch it. He pulls away from me and I can tell I'm bugging him. "I'm okay, Ruby!" he says. "Lemme alone."

"She's just trying to help," Ray says, which practically makes me fall over. It's the first time I've heard my brother defending me in ages.

"Let's get back home and I'll be fine!" Gary Daddy-o retorts. "It's just a flu. I already told you!"

Slowly by slowly, we trudge home in silence. I look up at the third-floor window, wondering how we're going to get Gary Daddy-o to climb the stairs. There's a man sitting on the stoop outside the building, and as we get closer, he waves at us. I don't wave back, because I don't know who he is and I'm really not in the mood for chatter right now.

Only by the time we get to the door, I recognize the man and let out a gasp. He's staring right at me and smiling, and he's got an envelope in his hand. It's Mr. Z. *What's he doing here?*

I stop, and we all stop.

"Hello, Ruby," Mr. Z says.

My throat is dry and cracked, but I know I have to

say something. I look at the envelope in Mr. Z's hand and then back at his smiling eyes.

"What are you—sorry," I say. "I mean—I mean. Hello."

22

KITTY

"RUTH TOLD ME you're staying here," Mr. Z says. "I hope I'm not interrupting."

"You're fine," Ray says.

"Well, good," Mr. Z replies. "I brought your pay, since you forgot to collect it."

"Thank you," I say, wondering why in the world Mr. Z would come out to deliver pay for a worker who was at his store a couple weeks over Christmas. I want to ask him, but of course I can't.

Ray holds out his hand to Mr. Z. "I'm Ruby's brother Ray."

Mr. Z shakes my brother's hand and says, "I thought so. You were there last night, right?"

"Yup," Ray says. "And this is our dad."

Mr. Z reaches for my dad's hand, which shakes just the teeniest bit, but I don't think Mr. Z notices. Gary Daddy-o is pale as a ghost and I'm worried he'll throw up or something. But he stands there, leaning against the wall outside the door, trying to smile.

"Your daughter is amazing," Mr. Z is saying. "She pitched in like a pro at the store and we really needed her. I can't say enough about how great she was. If there's any chance she'll come out here again, we'd love to have her back with us."

"Thank you," Gary Daddy-o says, and this time he's smiling for real.

"I'd love to," I say, because I have to say something. Then Mr. Z turns away from Gary Daddy-o to me.

"I came here to ask you a question," he says.

"Uh, sure," I say, and my heart starts beating faster like it always does when it feels like something important is about to happen.

"I loved your poem last night," Mr. Z is saying, and now my heart is beating even faster because the last thing I want is for him to describe the poem I wrote about my dad, while my father is listening.

"It was tender and imaginative and truly lovely," Mr. Z adds. "And the rhythm. I loved that!"

At this point I can hardly think, talk, or move. It feels like my feet are glued to the ground.

"I'm thinking of publishing an anthology of different poets from the Inner Pages family, and I consider you one of us," Mr. Z is saying. "I know you're leaving soon, and had to ask if that's all right with you."

"Oh wow," I say, like a two-year-old. "I mean, yeah, I'm—thank you. I'd be—it's an honor. Thank you so much."

"My pleasure!" he says, and then Gary Daddy-o says he's a little peaked and has to go upstairs.

"I'm sorry—" Mr. Z begins and my dad raises his hand.

"It's fine, please. Keep talking," he says.

Ray unlocks the door and turns to take our father's arm, but Gary Daddy-o says, "I'm fine!" and walks inside. Ray follows him and as Gary Daddy-o shuffles forward, Ray manages to wave and close the door. I hope he takes Gary Daddy-o's arm to get him up the stairs, but hope is all I can do right now, with Mr. Z staring at me.

I look up at him. "That was incredible of you to come here."

"You're worth it," Mr. Z answers, and I can't help smiling at him. *Did he really just say that?* This is turning out to be the best and worst day of my life.

"I'd love to send you a copy once it's published," Mr. Z says. "Is there an address in New York?"

I manage to smile and nod.

He pulls out a pocket-sized notebook and pen and hands it to me. "Will you write it down?"

"Oh, sure!" I say.

"Fantastic," he says.

I write down my address and hand Mr. Z's notebook back to him, feeling like my feet are still stuck. "I have to tell you, I love Inner Pages," I say. "It's the coolest bookstore I've ever seen."

"I'll never get tired of hearing that," Mr. Z says.

"I'll figure out a way to get back here as soon as I can."

"I'd love that, too," says Mr. Z. "But I don't want to keep you. I'm glad I got to meet your father and brother."

"Me too," I say, and then he says he hopes he'll see me in a few months or so and to keep writing. I tell him I will.

"Promise?" he asks.

"Cross my heart and hope to die," I say, which isn't something I usually say since I've never gone to church or anything. Mr. Z laughs, and we shake hands, and then I watch him walk away. He's got a little bounce in his step, like bursts of energy are racing through him.

He stops walking, turns around to look at me, and waves again. I wave back at him furiously. I can't even believe he wants to publish my poetry. When he starts walking away again, I can finally move my feet and jump upward, trying as hard as I can not to scream. Then I hit the buzzer because I know the door locks right after you go inside, and I didn't bring my key today. They buzz me in and I take the stairs two at a time until I'm at the door to our apartment.

"Whoooo-eeee!" I scream as the door opens, since nobody bothered to lock it. Ray stands up from the couch where he's sitting with Gary Daddy-o and looks at me, shaking his head. I figure he's mad, but the last thing I want is to talk to him about it. Before I can say anything, Gary Daddy-o starts applauding us from the couch.

"You did it, Ruby," says Ray, and I look up at him, surprised.

"You liked what I wrote?"

"You're an artist," Ray says, and I think he's trying to say something nice without telling Gary Daddy-o exactly what I wrote. "You care about what you're writing, and I like that."

"What did you write?" asks Gary Daddy-o.

"Just a poem about being a kid," I say, hoping that's enough for Gary Daddy-o right now.

"Well, good for you, honey," Gary Daddy-o says. I thank him, but when he starts to stand up, I can see his hands are still shaking. I rush over to him, and Ray and I help him stand. "I need a little rest," he mutters. "I'm going to lay down."

"Of course," I say. Ray and I walk him to his room and he gets into the bed like it's a life raft. I tell him I'll be back to check on him a little later and make him some tea.

"I'll be up later," he says. It seems like that's all he's been saying for the last two weeks.

"Okay," I tell him. Ray and I walk out of his bedroom and I close the door. Ray asks me what I want for dinner and says we've got a little chicken left over from our last trip to the store.

"Sure," I say. "Whatever's easiest."

"You know what?" he says. "I think you should call Nell."

"What for?" I ask.

"She's going to be happy for you."

"You think so?"

"I know it," Ray says. "She'll be proud of you, too."

I walk over to the phone and start dialing. It rings seven times before Nell-mom picks up the receiver.

"Hello?"

"It's Ruby," I say.

"Uh-oh," Nell-mom replies. "Are you going to be late again?"

"Nope," I say. "We're still coming back day after tomorrow. But something happened, and Ray thought I should tell you about it."

"Oh…kay," she says, and I can tell she thinks it's something bad. I tell her about Mr. Z and the poem, and her voice grows warm as she replies.

"You're kidding! That's fantastic!"

"What is it?" Chaz pipes in from the background.

"Hold on," she says to him, and then speaks into the phone. "Rubes, I'm so proud of you!"

"Thanks," I say, laughing. "That's exactly what Gary Daddy-o said."

"I hope so!" she says. "You're going to be a published poet. And you're not even thirteen!"

"I guess all those notebooks you bought me really helped," I say. "And thank you."

"I was happy to get them," says Nell-mom.

"No, I mean thank you for everything. For believing in me," I say.

"Oh, Ruby," she says, and her voice catches like she's trying to stop herself from crying. "Of course I believe in you. I always have and always will."

"And I don't think you should ever quit painting," I say. "You're an incredibly talented painter and you can't let anyone tell you otherwise. You just have to keep getting up every day and being an artist. Because I believe in you, too—and so does Ray."

"Oh, Ruby, if you knew what that means to me," she says, and this time I can really hear the tears in her voice. "You are the most incredible daughter in the whole world. I hope you know that."

Now it's my turn to almost cry. "I love you, Mom," I say, because it's mostly all I *can* say. I know the rest of the day will pass quickly, with bringing Gary Daddy-o tea and eating dinner and reading and stuff. I'll mostly think about what Mr. Z said, but I'll also be thinking about Nell-mom and how I've been with her, keeping my distance. I kept seeing all the stuff that made me mad, but not the good stuff she did that made my life better.

"I really, really love you," I say.

"I really, really love you right back, Kitty," she says, and I almost fall over. Kitty is the nickname she gave me when I was a little child, and she's the only one who ever used it.

"Thank you," I say.

"Lemme talk to Ray," she says, and I hand over the phone. Ray and Nell-mom talk for a few minutes and then he hangs up.

"That was cool," he says.

"Were you listening in on me?" I ask, frowning.

"I overheard without listening," he says, and we laugh. Maybe hearing me in such a good conversation with Nell-mom makes him like my poem a little better. Who knows?

Before we scarf down dinner, we set up chairs by the window, which is facing west so we can see the sun going down. It's almost like a necklace, with bands of red, yellow, and blue as it slowly sinks behind the buildings across the street.

Gary Daddy-o doesn't want any tea and seems to be getting worse. I ask if we should call a doctor, but he hates that idea.

"It has to be some kind of bug or something," he says. "You need to stay away and just bring me a glass and a pitcher of water."

I probably should stay away, since we're going to be traveling soon, but I hate to do it. Gary Daddy-o wins this one, though, and I bring him some water and then leave the room and close his door.

Ray finds a brownie and we split it for dessert.

Things are getting quiet enough so I can think about everything that happened the last few days. Mostly I'm thinking about Nell-mom coming to New York City from Sheboygan, Wisconsin, when she was barely sixteen years old. I think about her wanting to be an artist and telling her folks back home she'd write, and boarding a bus.

I know she and her little brother lived with their grandmother a while and when she died, the kids went to stay with an uncle. Maybe he told her not to be afraid to come home if things didn't work out. Did he slip her some money right before she got on the bus?

Or maybe he was mad at her for leaving, I don't know. She never talks about it except to say she was glad to find Chaz had moved to New York, too, though it was a surprise to both of them.

I just think Nell-mom must have wanted to be an artist really badly, because she says it's a hard life and you really have to want it. You have to deal with a lot of people saying "No!" and once in a while, saying, "Okay," or "Yes," or "Maybe." It could be that today was one of the few times in my life I'm going to hear a "yes," and I just have to be ready for that, to be tough and have a thick skin. All of that is what Nell-mom taught me to do.

A groan comes from Gary Daddy-o's room and I jump up to see if he's okay. I try to open the door but he's locked it.

"Gary Daddy-o? What's going on?"

He doesn't answer, but groans again. I pound on the door and somehow, it opens.

He's lying on the bed, completely drenched in sweat.

"You look really sick! We need to call someone!" I say.

"No doctor, now get *out* of here!" he says, frowning. "I told you to stay *away* from me!"

"What about taking your temperature?" I ask. "Isn't there a thermometer around here?"

"Ruby, I told you," Gary Daddy-o says through gritted teeth. "Get out of here."

Ray is standing in the doorway.

"Let's leave him for a little bit," he says. "If he's still feeling bad in the morning, we'll get a doctor."

"Not that we know anyone!" I say, and this time it's my turn to grit my teeth.

"We'll ask Marty's mom," Ray says, which I have to admit is not a bad idea.

"You get two more hours," I tell Gary Daddy-o. "I'm not waiting until morning."

He salutes me like a soldier and turns on his side. I pour him some water and leave the room, closing the door very gently.

Ray and I play a few games of checkers and I find myself getting sleepy. It's only seven-thirty, but I can't seem to keep my eyes open and tell Ray good night. "I'm just going to lay down for a little while and wake up to check on Gary Daddy-o."

Ray says he's right behind me, and even though it's never happened before I'm practically in dreamland when my head hits the pillow.

Only the dreams are all nightmares about Gary Daddy-o, who won't stop groaning in his sleep.

23

ANGEL AGAIN

I WAKE UP to the sound of the buzzer downstairs. I jump up and call out to Gary Daddy-o. He says, "Yeah, what?" but when I try his door, it's locked and he won't come out. The buzzer rings again. I know it's Les and Bo, but ask anyway and once I hear their voices, I let them in.

I can see the top of Bo's head coming upstairs and I've never been so happy to see anyone—except Les, maybe. We all hug and start chitter-chattering. They had a friend who was driving to San Francisco, so they didn't even have to take the train.

Bo asks how Gary Daddy-o's doing, and I tell them about the groaning and flu when Gary Daddy-o appears, leaning up against the door of his room in his pajama bottoms.

"Hey, man!" Bo says, and walks over to hug him. Gary Daddy-o looks straight at me and says, "What's going on?"

"We just couldn't pass up a trip to San Francisco," Les says. "It seemed like a great place to ring in the New Year, and here we are."

Gary Daddy-o keeps looking at me, without saying anything.

"You have breakfast yet?" says Bo. "We can go out and grab something—"

"We've got eggs and stuff right here," says Ray.

"Even better," says Les. "Maybe we can eat and play something. I mean—"

He doesn't finish because Gary Daddy-o's doubled over, crouching on the floor.

"Whoa!" says Les, and Bo kneels down in front of Gary Daddy-o.

"You all right, man? Should we call a doctor?"

"Leave me alone," Gary Daddy-o groans. "I know she must have called you."

"Let's get you back in bed," Bo says.

Gary Daddy-o is sweating so bad it looks like he's in the shower. Les and Bo get him up, but it takes a while and leaves them sweating, too. I try to come inside the bedroom, but Bo holds up a hand and blocks my way.

"Let me see what's going on here," he says. "We'll be out soon."

Ray goes back to the living room, and I follow him. Instead of sitting on the couch, Ray sits on the floor in front of it, right where we found Gary Daddy-o when we first got here. I'm wearing the same thing I had on yesterday and decide to change. By the time I'm done, I can hear Ray in the shower. Les and Bo are talking to Gary Daddy-o in his room, but I can't hear what they're saying.

Once Ray gets out of the shower, I decide that's what I need, too. By the time I'm dressed again, I can see Les and Bo in the kitchen. Les is making some toast, and Bo is drinking some water. He calls me over and sits down at the kitchen table.

"Come here, honey," Bo says. "We need to talk to you and Ray."

We sit down at the table, but my heart is going a mile a minute and I don't know if I'll be able to listen to a word Bo says.

"He's really sick, isn't he?" I say, because I don't want Les and Bo to pretend everything's fine when it isn't.

"Well, the news is actually better than you think," Bo says. "He does have a fever and chills, and it's going to get worse before it gets better. It feels like a flu to him, but the truth is—yeah."

Bo pauses, and Les looks at him and then us.

"What?" I say. "What's the truth?"

"Your dad's trying to give up drinking," Bo says. "If you drink liquor every day, it's hard to stop, and you feel sick when you do it—which is why most people don't want to do it."

"So—I don't get it," I say.

"He's been drinking a really long time, Ruby," says Ray.

"Exactly," says Bo. "And I think he knows it's way

past time for him to stop."

"And it makes him sick like this?" I ask. "Can't we help him feel better?"

"I wish we could, but we can't," Bo replies. "The best we can do is stay with him—which is what Les and I are going to do."

"Sorry, Bo, but he's our dad. We should be the ones staying."

Bo shakes his head. "I don't want you to stay. I don't think he wants it, either."

"I'm not going to leave him like this."

"Ruby," Les starts to say, but I turn on him, even though I don't mean to.

"No!"

"Listen, honey," Bo continues. "Your daddy doesn't want you to see him feeling this way and you have to respect that. Les and I are here to be with him, and you promised your mama you'd come home soon, right? You have to keep that promise or else your Nell-mom's going to be mad at me and Les. Understand?"

I try to nod as a tear rolls down my cheek. Bo grabs me and we hug, which makes more tears come out. Ray puts his hand on my shoulder and Les pats Ray on the arm. I can hear Gary Daddy-o groaning again, but Bo takes my face in his hands and keeps talking.

"See, I didn't know what I was going to find here," he explains. "Could've been a million things, but the best thing as far as I'm concerned is your dad trying to stop drinking. It looks bad, it looks really bad. But it means he's trying to change, and that means he wants to. Which is the only way *anything* changes—when the person wants it. D'you understand?"

"Yeah," I say, wiping my nose. Les pulls a handkerchief out of his pocket and hands it to me. I blow my nose and apologize.

"Don't be silly," Les says. "That's what handkerchiefs are for."

"So yeah, maybe we can have a little lunch and then Les'll take you to the train station," Bo says.

"We can go on our own," I tell him.

"I know, but we want to be sure everything goes all right," says Bo. "Just let me have my way on this one, okay?"

"Okay," I say, wondering why Ray hasn't said anything. Maybe he knew Gary Daddy-o was trying to stop drinking and just didn't want to tell me? That's the thing with brothers, they just barely talk to you. Especially when you need to know what's going on.

"Your brother misses his girl a lot, too," says Bo, as if he could read my mind. "It's just time for the two of you to get home."

"What happens when he's feeling better?" I ask. "Can he come home, too?"

"I don't know, Ruby, but—tell you what. We're going to figure that out."

"Yeah?"

"I promise," says Bo, and I want to tell him there's only one person in the world I'd believe right now, and that's him. And, of course, Les.

"The hard thing is, you're going to have to say goodbye to him after lunch," Bo says, and my heart starts pounding again as I stare at Bo. "I can't do that."

"Have to."

"He'll feel like we're leaving him—"

"Nope. It's exactly what he wants you to do. He wants—next time you see him, he wants to be feeling like himself again."

"I don't want lunch," I say, standing up and moving toward the window.

"We'll just pack something up for you," Bo says, and Ray says he'll put together some sandwiches.

Ray walks over to the refrigerator, and then the door to Gary Daddy-o's room opens. I hear him in the bathroom, and it sounds like he's sick again.

"I'll go help your dad," Bo says. "You want to start packing? Both of you."

The next hour is kind of a blur: packing, listening to Gary Daddy-o moaning and being sick, watching Ray and Les talk softly while Ray makes lunch, seeing Bo disappear into the bathroom and helping Gary Daddy-o lie down when they come out. For some reason, I think about Angel, because she seems like the kind of kid who would have seen this stuff. Marty wouldn't, for sure.

I sit on the couch with my head in my hands, trying to decide what, if anything, I can say to my father.

Les sits down next to me and I look up at him.

"You okay?" he asks.

"No."

"I get it," he says. "You know, sometimes life deals you a really bad hand. But if you have good friends, they can help you sort it out, Ruby, and that's why we came here. It won't all get better at once—it never does. But we're going to try as hard as we can to turn it all around. Okay?"

I nod, because there's a lump in my throat that won't let me talk anymore. I know I need to say something to Gary Daddy-o. I just don't know what.

I see Ray going into Gary Daddy-o's room and hear them murmuring to each other. I walk to the door of my dad's room and watch Ray leaning over the bed, hugging my dad. After a minute, Ray lets go and leaves the room, his face crumpling.

I walk to Gary Daddy-o's bed and he looks up at me, one eye open and one eye closed. "You look terrible," I say. He smiles.

"I always count on you to be honest, Ruby," Gary Daddy-o says, except when he says it, the word "always" sounds like "O-ways." And just hearing that very Gary Daddy-o word makes me feel like maybe, just maybe— he'll be all right.

We sit in silence for a little while and then he says, "Mad at me?"

"Kinda sorta," I say. "But I still love you, Gary Daddy-o."

"I love you, too," he replies. "I know how hard you tried to make me feel better, Rubes. And you know what? You did, and you also got me through Christmas—you and Ray. And I'm really lucky to have such incredible kids."

"I know that," I say. I take his hand and tell him how much I loved seeing him. Then I tell him I really want him to come back to New York and not stay in San Francisco.

"But then how are you going to see Mr. Z again at the bookstore?" he asks.

"We'll figure it out," I say. Gary Daddy-o nods and closes his eyes.

"I need to be alone for a while, baby," he says. I'm about to walk out when he grabs my hand, and I turn back to him. He kisses each knuckle, and then lets me go.

Les is waiting at the door with our suitcases by the time I leave the room, and I decide then and there I'm not going to cry right now. I hug Bo goodbye and thank him. "You're my hero today," I say.

"Mine too," Ray says.

Bo says we're *his* heroes, and then Les takes my suitcase and Ray takes his own. We head downstairs and I say goodbye to the city silently while we're walking to the bus. Part of me has a feeling I'll be back—at least to the bookstore that brought me the most fun I had here.

Les tells us that instead of a bus, he wants to spring for a cab, and knowing he comes from a rich family makes it easier to say yes. We flag down a taxi driving by on Columbus, and I wave at the Inner Pages window, thinking I can hardly wait to see my poem in the book Mr. Z publishes.

The streets aren't as crowded as they were before Christmas in North Beach, and the air is a little colder, too. On the way to the station in Oakland across the bridge, I start looking forward to getting back to Greenwich Village. Ray can see his girlfriend Jo-Jo. I can meet up with Sophie again, and let her know I'm not mad at her for getting close to my friend Michael. I won't say it right out, but she'll know it. That's how it is between Sophie and me.

"I don't want you to worry any more. Your worry time is done," Les says, and I'd bet anything he and Ray have been talking. And even though I got almost everything I wanted when Mr. Z said he wanted to publish my poem, none of it would matter without Bo and Les coming out here to help Gary Daddy-o and without Nell-mom and even Chaz and all our friends.

Once we're at the station, Les pays the driver. I half expect to see Angel and the other two boys we ran into on the first day we were here, but they're nowhere to be found. I think of Gary Daddy-o in his room feeling sick and wonder how long it'll take before he feels better.

Les pays for our tickets and stays with us until we board the train. We wave goodbye and he waves back, and as the train pulls out of the station, I think I see Angel, but when I wave, she doesn't see me and when I look closer I see the chick I'm looking at isn't Angel at all.

I close my eyes halfway, like Ruth told me to do, and try to see Angel in my own light, like painters do in their minds. I think about all the Beats around Inner Pages, and how Angel is a kind of Beat, too, because she walked all the way to Inner Pages to return my notebook. Maybe that means the people who say poems are useless are wrong, even if poetry isn't practical like bikes or buildings. Because if Angel hated my writing, she would have thrown the notebook out. Instead, she wanted to find me, even if it meant she'd get in trouble. Or maybe that's just the way I want to see her. You know?

And what if Gary Daddy-o reads my poem when Inner Pages publishes it and decides to come back to New York? I mean, it's possible, right? If someone really misses you.

The train chugs forward and I think I'll just stay here awhile, looking out the window and saying goodbye to California. Everywhere I look, there's light.

READER'S GUIDE

IF YOU'VE READ the first and second books in this series, you already know it's set in New York. In this third and final book of the Beat Street Series, I brought the action out to San Francisco, California, where a substantial number of Beats gathered, in addition to those who lived in New York.

The fun part about setting the story in San Francisco involves introducing Ruby and her brother to a whole new world. The North Beach neighborhood of San Francisco, where the siblings' father is staying, is full of surprises—including much warmer weather than you'd find in New York in December.

I titled the book *North Beat Christmas* because the story, which happens during the Christmas season, is also very connected to the Beat culture that surrounds it—as numerous Beat poets were living in North Beach in 1958. Although Christmas is supposed to be one of America's happiest holidays, the season is a difficult one for Ruby. She and her brother are forced to deal with their father's addiction to alcohol, and don't have the tools to do that—like most people their age.

I wrote *North Beat Christmas* not only for middle-grade kids and teens struggling with family issues, but for those who live in healthier families who want to learn more about struggles like these. I wish I could say there are easy answers, but I can't.

What I can say is that Ruby finds a way to feel better by reading and writing poetry, working at a famous local bookstore, and meeting the people who work there and visit. In past books, Ruby has also turned to art to make her feel better and less alone; in this book, it is what helps her to survive.

To learn more about the poets Ruby loved, see if you can find poetry by writers including Charles Bukowski, Gregory Corso, Allen Ginsberg, Jack Kerouac, Denise Levertov, Kenneth Patchen, and Marie Ponsot. If you can get to San Francisco, you'll likely find echoes of the Beat Generation in North Beach—and a whole lot more.

QUESTIONS FOR DISCUSSION

1. In the opening chapter, Ruby shares her worries about her father being depressed and drinking alcohol. Knowing adults can drink too much, why is she so worried? What does she think will happen to her father if he drinks alot?

2. Both Ruby and her brother Ray have a strong relationship with their father's friends Les and Bo. What role do they play in the siblings' lives? What do you think would happen to Ruby's family without them?

3. Ruby and Ray pride themselves on being careful when they travel. Yet when they arrive in San Francisco, they meet a group of teens who steal some of Ruby's belongings. Was there anything they could have done to keep it from happening?

4. Throughout the book, Gary Daddy-o's addiction damages Ruby's and Ray's ability to celebrate Christmas. Yet, brother and sister each try in their own ways to help their father drink less and enjoy the season more. Do you think they succeed or fail?

5. One of the best things that happens to Ruby while she is in California is getting hired at a bookstore. How does working there make a difference in Ruby's life?

6. What does Ruby learn from her relationship with Ruth, who oversees Ruby at Inner Pages?

7. Ruby also meets a boy her own age named Marty, who comes to the bookstore, often with his mom. Marty is different from anyone Ruby knows, and it takes her a while to understand him. How does her friendship with Marty teach Ruby about differences and accepting people for who they are?

8. How do Ruby and Ray differ in their responses to their father in this book?

9. What is Ruby trying to say in the poem she reads at Inner Pages?

10. Will Ruby's relationship with *her mom* improve after what she's seen and learned during her Christmas holiday?

ABOUT THE AUTHOR

JENNA ZARK IS an award-winning author and playwright. Her most recent book *Crooked Lines* earned six awards and honors, including first prize for a memoir in the Overcoming Adversity/Tragedy Category from the Next Generation Indie Book Awards and the Silver Award in the Religious Spiritual Category from the Nautilus Book Awards. Zark is also the author of two middle-grade books: *The Beat on Ruby's Street* and *Fool's Errand. The Beat on Ruby's Street* won first prize from Wishing Shelf awards in the UK and was a finalist for the Minnesota Author's Project. Zark's play *A Body of Water* was published by Dramatists Play Service, and produced at Circle Repertory Company in New York. To learn more, visit jennazark.com, and while you're there, sign up for her newsletter—it's a great way to keep in touch.